Daddy's Assistant

A DDLG and ABDL erotic story about a Daddy Dom who trains his assistant to be his sexy baby girl

By Tina Moore

Table of Contents

Chapter 1

Amber groaned as she tapped on her phone, calculating the final total for this month's bills, and put her head down despondently on the table.

"Is it really that bad?" Asked her roommate Leslie sympathetically. Amber only groaned again and nodded, pushing the phone in her direction. Leslie took a peek at the total on the calculator app on Amber's phone. It was enough to make even her wince. Not that Leslie was well off or anything, but she was at least steadily employed, which was more than Amber could say.

"Yikes. That's per person?" Leslie asked. Amber sighed and sat up. She scanned their threadbare apartment for anything she might be able to sell, but there was nothing left of any value. Handmade quilts gifted to you by your Aunt Betty weren't exactly top-ticket items, or so she had been told by several pawnshop owners.

Everything else had been sold off already. It had been so long since she'd had any acting gig, much less a paying one, and all of her savings had dried up months ago.

"Yep," Amber replied as she downed the remainder of tea in her chipped mug and poured more hot water over the tea bag, steeping it for a second time. Pretty soon, she wouldn't be able to afford tea at all if things kept up this way.

"Sorry, hun," said Leslie.

"But that's going just about to wipe me out. I won't be able to loan you any more money this month," she added. Amber looked at her with guilt all over her face. It wasn't fair of her to keep borrowing money from her roommate, anyway. Leslie had problems of her own without Amber adding to them. She appreciated that Leslie had never tried to make her feel bad about not having enough money, but that didn't mean that it was ok for her to take advantage of that. She needed to figure out a more permanent solution.

"Fair enough. It's fine. I'll manage, don't

worry about me. I have lots of plasma to sell," Amber replied.

"Look," Leslie sat down beside her at their small table, putting her hand over Amber's in a show of support.

"Why don't you get a temporary job?" Leslie offered.

"I know that I should, it's just that it feels so much like giving up. I came to the city to be an actress, not to be a waitress or gas attendant. I know I shouldn't expect to be famous overnight and that I have bills to pay. But at the same time, if I get a job, I might miss out on auditions. Also, I'm really a terrible waitress. I mean, just awful," Amber said with her head between her hands.

"I know, and that does suck but think of it like this. Would you really enjoy a summer of eating ramen and getting your plasma sucked out three times a week? How good would you really be in an audition with malnutrition and blood loss?" Leslie said. Amber managed a chuckle even as her shoulders sagged in defeat.

"No, I guess you're right. I'll hit up Craigslist, see what I can find," Amber said, sitting up. Leslie patted her hand consolingly and got up to retreat back to her spot in front of the television.

"Chin up. Maybe you can find something really chill," she said hopefully as she went to settle back down with her snacks. Amber hoped that she was right. Acting gigs were few and far between and seldom paid well. She had worked in retail and foodservice but found that she was far too anxious for that line of work. One angry word from a customer would rattle around in her head for days, and given her ineptitude in those areas, she heard a lot of angry words. Everything else that she had applied for had wanted years of experience that she didn't have, even the so-called entry-level positions. It was tough out there, no matter what line of work you were in. It would seem.

She opened her laptop and did a broad search, quickly eliminating jobs that paid too little or had requirements that she didn't meet. One job, in particular, did look promising, however, a call for a personal assistant. *Seeking candidates with unusual levels of loyalty and devotion to their employer.* She pondered that for a moment, assuming they meant long hours with little pay. However, as she read through the advertisement, she noticed that the pay per hour listed was very impressive. There were very few details other than that to give her a clue as to what she might expect. Burning with curiosity, she replied to the email and attached her resume, then continued her search.

Nothing would probably come of it, she thought, *just like dozens of other applications that never get answered.* But if it did, she could certainly get used to that kind of money! She dreamed of paying Leslie back and saving enough money to once again rededicate herself to her craft. She cautioned herself against getting her hopes up but found herself dreaming about it anyway.

Malcolm sifted through a pile of resumes, bored with the task of finding a personal assistant for himself. This was the sort of thing that he used to delegate to Natasha before she had selfishly decided to abandon him.

You know that's not fair, he chided himself. Natasha had found the man of her dreams over the holidays, living right next door to her parents of all places, and decided to move halfway across the country to be with him. While Malcolm was happy for her if somewhat begrudgingly, it did leave him in a bit of a pickle, he doubted that he would find another assistant who was half as capable as Natasha had been. She was whip-smart, beautiful, and catered to his every whim, sexual and otherwise. Best of all, she followed his number one rule: don't fall in love. He preferred to keep things as professional as possible. He didn't have time for the messy emotional entanglements that come with dating and did not like the idea of hiring a prostitute, so he had found that striking up a certain arrangement with his personal assistants was the best course of action in that department.

It had taken a few false starts before he had found the perfect combination of competence and obedience in Natasha, and he loathed the thought of having to go through the process all over again. What were the chances of finding another Natasha? Truly that girl had been one in a million. Wearily, he checked his messages and to his surprise, saw a rather promising email in response to his online ad. He quickly looked the candidate up on social media and saw that she was pretty, young, and almost heartbreakingly naive looking. He could feel himself respond to her picture immediately, blood rushing to his cock as soon as he saw her smile, wide and innocent. This one would be worth meeting, certainly. She would look so sexy kneeling before him with only a diaper on and a collar around her neck. He typed out a quick reply, specifying the time and place that he expected her to meet him, already dreaming of keeping her under his desk to pleasure him any time he wanted. Her innocent smile made him want to corrupt her to make her his completely. It had only been a few days since Natasha moved out, and already his sex drive was through the roof. He checked the application again and saw that this new girl's name was Amber. He closed his eyes and thought about tying up sweet Amber, forcing orgasm after orgasm onto her helpless body until she was a drooling, babbling mess. He could tell just by looking at her that this one would require quite a bit of training, which he very much looked forward to giving it to her.

He pulled his cock out, stroking it fiercely as he imagined throat training her. He would keep her in a diaper and collar, nothing else, as he taught her how to deepthroat him. He didn't mind admitting that he had a huge cock, and most women struggled when it came to giving him head. When he got through with sweet, little Amber, however, she would swallow him down like the well-trained whore he hoped her to become. He ached to fondle her perfect perky breasts as she choked on him, taking every inch of him down her bulging throat. A ragged sigh escaped his lips as he furiously jerked himself, enjoying the mental image. She almost certainly had never had a Daddy, and he looked forward to showing her all of the fun that could be had. She would look so cute begging for his cum, begging him to fuck her. Most of all, she would look so cute cumming all over his cock. He wanted to make all of her worries melt away, to her the luxury of thinking only about surrendering to his pleasure. As he thought of making her his princess, he erupted jizz all over his hands and pants, wishing it was filling up Amber's tight little pussy instead. She would be his, he vowed. She would be his very soon.

Chapter 2

Amber ran down the sidewalk breathlessly, clutching a scrap of paper that had the correct time and address hurriedly scrawled on it. She couldn't afford a cab ride across town, and so she decided to leave early enough to walk. It was a very long walk, taking her hours. Somewhere along the way, she had gotten a bit lost, however, and was having to really hustle to make it on time. At last, she found the correct building number, confirming with the doorman that Mr. Graham did, in fact, live there. She breathed a sigh of relief, as it looked as though she would actually make it on time, even if just barely. Once inside the elevator, she punched in the floor and the security code he had given her. To her surprise, the elevator opened up to a living space. She stepped forward tentatively into the nicest apartment she had ever seen, peeking around the corners to see if she saw anyone.

"Hello?" she called out but didn't hear a response. She stepped further into the room and craned her neck to peek up the stairs. She heard noises, so she stepped onto the bottom stair, trying to get close enough to hear what was going on without intruding.

"Oh, Daddy," she heard a female voice saying.

"Yeah, fuck me with that big dick, Daddy!" Came the voice, making Amber's eyes go wide. Amber gasped and felt her face growing hot. She ran back toward the elevator, not sure what she should do. Her instinct was to run away and hide, feeling like she had violated someone's privacy somehow. But, as she reached out for the elevator button, she stopped herself. She was at the correct location at the correct time. The security code wouldn't have worked if she had punched in the wrong floor by mistake. If she had interrupted something, that was hardly her fault. She smoothed her hair and skirt to compose herself once more and sat on the couch, as far away from the stairs as physically possible, and decided to wait as long as it took. She tried to tune out the sex noises, but they certainly weren't making it easy. She heard moans and loud smacks and a steady thumping. As it seemed to go on and on, she found herself getting a little heated herself.

Wildly inappropriate, she chided herself. Still, it seemed as though the two of them were having a marvelous time, and she found herself to be a little jealous. It had been quite some time since she had been on a date. Trying to be an actress took up so much of her time and energy that it didn't leave much room for anything else. Even when she had had sex last, it wasn't nearly as much fun as whatever these two were getting up to. The guy, Greg she thought his name was, had been very nice but very boring. He didn't exactly make her see fireworks, and she never retook his calls. At last, the two seemed to finish up, their climatic moans echoing throughout the entire apartment. Amber cleared her throat and straightened her blazer, trying her best to ignore the heat between her legs.

Ten minutes later, a woman descended the stairs, a young brunette in a pants suit similar to Amber's. She nodded politely to Amber on her way out but otherwise didn't acknowledge her. The woman got on the elevator and left, and still, Amber waited. She was on the verge of leaving when, at last, a man in a pair of black slacks and a crisp, white shirt came down the stairs. He was easily the most handsome man she had ever seen, with dark hair, dark eyes, and five o'clock shadow sprinkled over a rugged jawline. He spotted her on the couch and didn't say anything for a moment, only put his hands in his pockets and looked her up and down appraisingly. The way that he assessed her was strangely arousing to her, something in the way that his eyes appeared hungry yet cold at the same time. She did her best not to flinch or blush but rather to meet his penetrating gaze with one of her own. Despite the fluttering in her stomach, she somehow succeeded.

"Ms. Bennet, you're early," he said at last. His voice was low and gravelly, sending pleasant tingles all through her. Despite his arrogant attitude, she found herself drawn to him. He had a dominance, a sort of gravitas about him, that she had never experienced before.

"I was exactly on time, actually," she corrected. Again, they just stared at each other, matching stoney gaze for stoney gaze. She was surprised by her own boldness. Normally, she wasn't one to challenge authority figures. But then, most authority figures didn't ignite some strange passion inside of her that she didn't fully understand. All that heat had to go somewhere, she supposed.

"Come," he said after studying her for a long moment and began to walk away without so much as looking back to see if she followed. She suppressed an eye roll at his continued rudeness and followed him to his office. As he poured himself a drink at the minibar, she sat in a chair opposite his desk and waited patiently.

"Would you care for a drink?" he asked.

"It's ten-thirty in the morning," she responded, careful to keep her tone even. He snapped his head around and glared at her anyway.

"I didn't ask you what time it is. I asked you if you wanted a drink." His tone was low and vaguely threatening, but she didn't let that rattle her. Or at least, it didn't intimidate her so much as it heightened her attraction to him. She found his dominant energy to be refreshingly stimulating. She was surprised at her own reaction, but it was so strong that it was impossible to fight it or deny it.

"No, thank you," she said, still keeping her tone polite. He sat down at his desk and took a sip of his drink before speaking.

"Ms. Bennet, I should start by saying that this is not your normal personal assistant position. I want to be very upfront about that. If it makes you uncomfortable or you don't think you can handle it, we will end this interview right now, no questions asked. If you believe that you can and want to fulfill my expectations, then we can proceed. Do you understand?" The handsome stranger asked.

"I understand. What exactly are these unusual expectations you speak of?" She replied nodding her head.

"First of all, I will require you to live here full time. I am a demanding employer, and I expect you to be at my beck and call twenty-four-seven. Secondly, I will require you to service me in every way possible." He leaned forward, watching her reaction closely, letting the words hang in the air. She picked up on the insinuation immediately but didn't react right away, not even so much as a raised eyebrow. She knew that she should be disgusted, that she should get her purse and leave in an indignant huff. She played the scene in her head, imagined the cutting words she would say, putting him in his place as she left him to wallow in his own lechery. She knew that's what she should do, but the curious tingle between her legs kept her in her chair and under his penetrating stare. She found that she didn't want to put him in his place but rather the other way around.

"You understand what I'm referring to, of course," he prompted when she didn't say anything for a while. She nodded slowly, feeling as if he had put her under some sort of trance or spell. She didn't understand where these thoughts or urges were coming from.

"Good," he purred. "I am a man of unusual tastes, and I require my partner to do whatever I say, whenever I say it, without question. This is true both in business and in the bedroom." Again, the alarm bells that were telling her to get out of there were far outweighed by the clenching heat she felt within her core as she thought about being under his command. Her breath quickened slightly, and she felt almost drunk. She swallowed, finding her voice at last.

"Your girlfriend doesn't object to this arrangement?" She was still somehow managing to keep an even tone of voice, as though they were having a perfectly normal conversation as if this were a perfectly normal job interview.

"I don't have a girlfriend. If you are referring to the young lady who just left, she is another candidate for the position. She was eager to show just how obedient she could be and wanted to audition. Don't worry about her, though. She wasn't up for some of my more unusual requests. I don't think I'll be hearing from her again." She swallowed hard, wondering what the deal-breaker had been and if she would be able to handle it any better. There was no way to know but to try, after all. She found that she was eager to prove herself to him. Even though she had just met him, she found herself wanting to make him proud.

"Will you be required me to ... audition as well?" she asked, almost afraid of the answer. Her eagerness was mixed with more than a little nervousness. This was all so new.

"Only if you want to, but I do not require it. I have a good feeling about you, Amber. You seem," he paused, taking in a deep breath as he looked her up and down again, his gaze lingering on her breasts. "Different. I believe you and I are going to get along quite well. However, why don't we each take the evening to think it over and touch base tomorrow? We wouldn't want to be too hasty, now would we?"

"Alright," she heard herself say distantly. Every time he gave her one of those intense looks, it turned her brain to jelly, and it became impossible to think straight. Perhaps it was wise to sleep on it. She stood on shaky legs and extended her hand to shake. He took it, rubbing his thumb over her palm, making her gasp quietly as a jolt of electric desire gripped her. He smiled arrogantly, almost a sneer. On any other man, it would have been offputting, but on him, it was a powerful aphrodisiac.

"Until we meet again," he said and kissed the back of her hand, holding her gaze as he did so. She nodded at him politely and left the room, unable to ignore the fact that her panties were soaking wet. She reserved the right to change her mind once her hormones had settled down, of course, but right then, she was leaning heavily towards a yes. The idea of giving her body over to this man was the most exciting thing to happen to her in quite some time.

Chapter 3

Amber found it almost impossible to sleep that evening, her conversation with Mr. Graham kept running over and over in her mind. As much as she knew she should reject his offer outright, she found that she actually wanted to accept it, even after his intoxicating influence had worn off. Something about him fascinated her, made her crave to be around him, to be his. Even his vague references to his dark desires left her both curious and titillated. The woman who had interviewed before her had been joyfully calling him Daddy, which was shocking enough to Amber's inexperienced sensibilities. Her mind raced as she wondered what it could have been that scared her off. She couldn't stop imagining fucking Mr. Graham, calling him Daddy in her mind as he pounded into her. Instead of being turned off by the taboo, she found it incredibly arousing and started rubbing herself over the top of her pajama pants. In her mind's eye, she saw his penetrating gaze, staring into her eyes as he held her down, pinning her wrists down over her head with his strong hands. She wondered what it would feel like to have him inside of her, to let him use her body however he wished like some kind of erotic plaything. It sounded so vulgar, and yet it made her so wet.

She slipped her hand under the waistband and started rubbing her clit frantically, shuddering as the pleasure intensified. "You're mine," she heard him say in her mind as he took her savagely. She found that she craved to belong to him, to serve him. It made her pussy throb to think of herself as being under his control. She pinched her nipples as she thought of his commanding energy and dominant tone of voice. Sometimes, late at night, she had fantasized about being someone's sexual plaything just as she was now, and only this time, there was a chance that it could actually become a reality. She wondered if he would keep her in chains or in some sort of elaborate sex dungeon. The thought of being bound and spread before him made her cum. Biting her lip to muffle her soft noises of pleasure, she quivered under her covers and then finally quieted, gasping and limp-bodied. In the cold light of the next morning, however, she once again doubted whether it was a good idea. If she was concerned about a part-time job not leaving her with enough time for acting, how would being a live-in personal assistant be any better?

On the other hand, the pay was so good she would be able to save money, especially if she sublet her room while she was working for him. Within a few months, she would have enough saved enough that she could focus only on acting for a while. As she was thinking it over, she heard her phone buzz.

I have decided that you will begin working for me tomorrow. A driver will arrive at your place at 9 AM sharp. Do not be late. Respond "Yes, Daddy" if you agree. Even in his texts, he was commanding.

She felt a surge of desire for him and knew that there was no way that she could turn down this opportunity.

Yes, Daddy. She smiled as she typed the words, already looking forward to her new life.

***

Amber spent the rest of the day packing her things. She explained to Leslie that her new job required her to be on call day and night. She decided that leaving out the more sordid details was probably prudent. Luckily, Leslie said that she knew of a co-worker who was hunting for a new place, and before the day was done, all of the details had been ironed out. Amber would move out tomorrow, and the new girl would move in the following day and take over her portion of the rent and utilities from that point on until further notice. Amber would leave her furniture behind for the other girl to use so she wouldn't have to rent a storage unit and only take her personal items with her to

Malcolm's. That evening, Amber found it difficult to sleep. She was so excited and nervous that not even masturbating could soothe her to sleep. Even after she made herself cum, she still ached for her new Daddy, as she was already calling him in her mind. Her mind raced as she tried to imagine what sort of kinky things he would want to do to her which only made her horny all over again. After a fitful night of tossing and turning, it was finally time to go to him.

She was waiting for the driver when he arrived, suspecting that he would not hesitate to tattle on her if she kept him waiting. What little she knew about Malcolm so far made her assume that he was going to be a very strict boss. The driver put her bags in the trunk and told her to help herself to any of the drinks or snacks, but Amber found that she was too nervous to eat and could not bring herself to pour a drink at nine in the morning even if it would calm her down. Funny how selling herself to a perfect stranger didn't make her blink an eye, but day drinking was a bridge too far. She stifled a giggled and shrugged at her own quirkiness. As they arrived at Mr. Graham's building, her bags were passed off to the doorman, who escorted her into the elevator as though she were some terribly important person. When the door opened again, Mr. Graham was waiting for them, again wearing perfectly tailored black slacks. His button-up was navy blue today, setting off his chocolate brown eyes perfectly. Just the mere sight of him instantly made Amber's body grow hot with desire. Without a word, he slipped the doorman some cash and took Amber's bags from him.

"Come," he said once they were alone again. "I will show you to your room." He led her up the stairs where she saw that his apartment was even larger than she had imagined. The room he had put aside for her was luxurious with a four-poster bed, a dresser, and vanity, even a gorgeous cherry wood bookcase filled with books of all sorts. She couldn't wait to get her hands on those books and hoped that she would have time to read as his assistant.

Mr. Graham put her bags on the floor and turned to face her. There was none of the coldness in his eyes that had been present at their first meeting. Now there was only pure, raw hunger as he looked her up and down. All thoughts left her mind as the air between them grew thick with electricity.

"From this moment on, you are mine. You will submit to me in every way. Is that understood?" She suppressed a shiver of excitement as his words filled her with a jolt of electric heat. It was unbelievable how aroused she had gotten just from that one sentence. He locked his eyes onto hers, and she was filled with a need to please him, to obey him. Slowly, she nodded her head.

"I'm afraid that's not good enough, sweet little Amber. I need to hear you say it, to make sure that you truly understand what I am asking of you." He stepped closer to her as he spoke, dominant confidence rolling off of him in waves, heightening her excitement and leaving her feeling more than a little dazed with lust.

"From this moment," she repeated dutifully. "I am yours. I will submit to you in every way." He smiled and stroked her face with the back of his hand. Surprised by the soft gesture, she let her eyes flutter closed for a moment, before opening them to find he was staring at her with an intensity that made her legs feel weak. The way he looked at made her feel like he could see directly into her mind.

"From now on, you will call me Daddy at all times." He was so close that his warm breath washed over her lips as he spoke. She yearned for him to close that distance and put his lips on hers, but she knew what he expected of her and knew that she must perform her duty.

"Yes, Daddy," she whispered, leaning into his heat with the hope that he would reward her good behavior with a kiss.

"Good," he said curtly and stepped back, breaking the spell. Her body cried out for him, but he quickly returned to a business-like manner, and the moment passed. "We have a lot of work to do today. The first order of business is to solidify our contract."

"Contract?" she asked, somewhat confused. He chuckled affectionately at the dumbfounded look on her face that was also mixed with a pouting disappointment.

"Yes, little one. It is vital that we both protect ourselves, legally speaking. I will allow you twenty minutes to unpack your things, and then you will meet me in my office downstairs. Is that clear?"

"Yes, Daddy," she said automatically, already allowing herself to slip into a submissive state of mind. It already felt so natural, as though she could deny him nothing.

"Good girl,' he said, making her body feel hotter, her need growing so intense that her body cried out for his touch. To her great disappointment, he only kissed her forehead lightly before leaving the room abruptly. She sat on the bed, her head spinning. That gentle gesture of kissing her on the forehead did not at all line up with his otherwise harsh demeanor, and it left her completely disoriented, wondering if she fully understood what was happening here after all. Suddenly, having everything written out in black and white seemed like a very good idea.

Chapter 4

She joined him downstairs at the specified time. It hadn't taken her long to unpack her things, and she had spent the rest of the time perusing the bookshelf, trying to decide which one she wanted to read first. When she came into his office, he already had a copy of the contract out on the desk ready for her to read. The contract was surprisingly vague, only covering legal liability while leaving her to wonder at the day-to-day specifics, much as she had done for days now. He explained all of the legalese to her patiently and put the whole thing in layman's terms. Basically, both parties were free to end the arrangement at any time with no questions asked, and both parties were barred from discussing any of the specifics with anyone else to protect their privacy. It did, however, provide her with a generous severance package should either of them decide that they wanted to end things, which surprised her. Nothing in the contract alarmed her, so Amber signed it right away, eager to get on with it. He slipped it into an envelope and placed it in his desk drawer.

"Now," he said matter of factly. "It is time to show you where you will be staying during your training period." Her brow wrinkled in confusion.

"I won't be staying in my room?" He leaned back in his chair, tenting his hands and staring at her for a moment. She knew that he was only doing it to make her squirm, but that didn't stop it from working. She longed to know what he was thinking when he looked at her that way: something filthy, no doubt.

"No," he said, once he had made her sufficiently uncomfortable. "You will have to earn that privilege. Follow me." With no further explanation, he took her back upstairs and led her to a room next to her bedroom. He stood by the door and gestured toward the handle.

"Go on," he prompted. With a shaky hand, she reached forward and opened the door slowly, her heart pounding with nervous anticipation. On the other side was a nursery or so it seemed. Upon closer inspection, however, it seemed that everything was adult-sized. The crib was as big as a twin-sized bed, and the changing station was enormous, big enough to comfortably fit a grown-up. She looked around at the sea of pastels and stuffed animals, more confused than ever. This was nothing like what she had expected to find. Still not explained, he went to the closet and opened it to reveal a long row of frilly dresses, choosing a light purple one from the rack. He lay the garment down on the changing table and pulled out an adult diaper from the built-in drawer, laying it on top of the dress. She couldn't tear her eyes away from the diaper. Surely he didn't expect her to wear one of those.

"Strip," he said commandingly. She blinked at him, flabbergasted.

"But - "

"Little girls don't argue," he said firmly. "Little girls do as they are told. Strip. I want to see what is mine." Something in his tone of voice stopped all of her objections in their tracks. Before she even knew what she was doing, she was lifting her shirt over her head. She began to hurriedly slide her skirt to the floor, but he stopped her with a gesture.

"Slower," he said, his eyes burning into her. Matching his stare, she let her hands slide down over the curves of her hips before peeling her skirt down slowly. He made a quiet noise of approval as the garment hit the floor, leaving her only in her underwear. He smirked as she undid the clasp of her bra, holding it place with her hands for a moment as she let the straps dangle, teasing him. As she let it drop to the floor along with her skirt, revealing her perky breasts, he drew a sharp breath, and the bulge in his pants grew more obvious. Lastly, she slid her panties down, showing him her freshly shaved pussy.

"That's better. Good girl," he purred as she

stood before him completely naked. "You are a very sexy young lady. For the duration of your training period, you will wear neither a bra nor panties. Only diapers and dresses from now on, is that understood?"

"Yes, Daddy," she said, feeling small and vulnerable. While she didn't fully understand, she found that her eagerness to serve outweighed her need to understand. He began to move towards her, slowly like a predatory cat who has spotted its prey. Holding her in his gaze, he reached out and casually stroked her breast, pinching her nipple lightly between his fingers. Her breath caught at the sensation of aching need that suddenly gripped her. He moved closer to her, close enough to kiss her, but again, he refrained. He lifted her up by her hips and put her on the changing table. She loved the way it felt to be handled by him, the way he lifted her up as though she weighed nothing. It made her feel like a delicate doll.

"Lay back," he instructed and positioned the diaper underneath her. With a practiced hand, he had the diaper in place and had it fastened within seconds.

"Up," he commanded and had her sit with her arms above her head so that he could put the dress on her. Once she was properly zipped up, he picked her up again and placed her back on her feet.

"Turn around," he said. "Slowly." She did a slow spin, mindful of his eyes on her as she let him look at her from every angle. He nodded in approval and bent down to retrieve something from another drawer.

"You look beautiful, princess, but there is just one thing missing." It was a box in his hand, and when he opened it, there was a pacifier inside. He took it from the box and laid it gently in her mouth.

"There. Now you are absolutely perfect."mHe kissed the handle of her pacifier, and she blushed.

Chapter 5

She had expected him to fuck her there and then, but he didn't. He took her downstairs to his office and gave her a brief overview of the business side of their relationship. He was a lawyer who worked primarily from home, but, as he explained, he would occasionally have to go into the office, much more rarely, so would she. He had a paralegal and a secretary for most of the things directly related to his law practice, he said. Most of what she would be doing was attending to his personal needs: errands, housework, scheduling, that kind of thing. Her mind was racing, but every time she started to ask a question, he put up a hand to stop her.

"Don't you worry your pretty little head about that right now. For the duration of your training period, you will not be expected to do anything other than learning how to be a perfect little girl for Daddy. That is your primary job until further notice," Her mind burned with further questions, but he only pushed to pacifier back in her mouth, effectively cutting off any further conversation. He made her lunch, making her sit in a highchair as she ate. She was sort of taken aback by that if anything she assumed she would be responsible for making their meals. He wouldn't even let her eat by herself, insisting on feeding her bite by bite. Everything was happening so quickly, and none of it was as she had expected it to be. None of it was unpleasant so far, just unexpected. He declared that after lunch, she would have to take a nap and she found herself to actually be grateful for the break. There was so much to process, and it was making her feel drained, even a little anxious. He carried her to the nursery and sat in a rocking chair with her in his lap. His arms engulfed her, warm and strong, and she found herself melting into him. He stroked her hair as he rocked her, and the comforting sensations soothed her frayed nerves. It felt so nice to forget about her questions and just let herself be babied for a while. The lack of sleep from the night before combined with the stress of the day caught up with her as she rested in his arms and she began to nod off. Despite how much she needed the rest, she found herself fighting it a little, not wanting to leave the bliss and safety of his arms, even for the sweet respite of sleep. Eventually, however, she gave in, and her heavy lids closed. He lifted her, slowly and gently, and she was just awake enough to register that he laid her down in the crib, covered her with a blanket, and kissed her on the forehead.

"Sleep tight, baby girl," he whispered and tiptoed out of the room.

***

When she awoke from her nap, she felt refreshed and energized. She sat up to see that the crib had her essentially locked in. She could get out if she really needed to in an emergency, but for the most part, she was stuck. As she stretched and wiped the sleep from her eyes, she noticed that she had to use the bathroom. She looked around the room, spotting a baby monitor on the dresser.

"Daddy?" she called out tentatively, not sure if the thing was even on. Sure enough, he came into the room just a few moments later.

"Well, hello, princess," he said fondly as he approached the crib. "Did you have a nice nap?"

"Yes, it was nice, thank you. I need to go to the bathroom, can you let me out?" He shook his head.

"No. You can get out of your crib if you want, but potties are for big girls. Little girls use their diapers." She froze and stared at him, not sure if she had heard him correctly. Did he really expect her to pee herself? Wearing a diaper was one thing; she was happy to play along if that pleased him in some way. But the thought of wetting herself made her burn with embarrassment.

"What? What do you mean?" She hoped

beyond hope that she had misunderstood, that there was some other explanation.

"Exactly what I said, little one. You go potty in your diaper from now on. Are you going to do what Daddy says, or am I going to have to spank you?" She could tell that from the tone in his voice that it wouldn't be the kind of playful, sexy spanking that she heard people talk about from time to time. She had a feeling that he would make sure that she wouldn't like the spanking that he gave her one little bit. She squirmed, the need to urinate only growing stronger. The last thing she wanted was to screw this up on her very first day. Even more than that, she didn't want to disappoint him.

"Ok, Daddy," she said. "I'll try." Try as she might, however, not a drop would come out. She seemed to have some sort of mental block against it. Her heart plummeted as he scowled at her, his anger feeling like the most devastating thing in the world. She could feel the tears begin to spring to her eyes, blurring her vision. "I- I can't ..." He looked at her with a strange combination of emotions on his face. He looked like he was about to say something, but didn't. As he finally started to move toward her, she flinched away from him.

"There, there, little one," he said, putting a comforting hand on her shoulder. "Daddy isn't angry. I know you tried. This is for your own good, to help you learn and grow. Understand?" She didn't really understand, but she knew that he didn't want her to be afraid, so she sniffled and nodded anyway, putting on a brave face. He took her hand and led her to the bed, where he sat. He suddenly seemed much more imposing to her, as if he had grown a few inches in the last few seconds but she knew that was only a result of her fear and shame.

"Over my lap," he said firmly but gently. Her eyes were still streaming with tears, but she complied, laying herself over his firm thighs. It was uncomfortable to have the full weight of her body pressing on her overfull bladder and made the urge to go that much more intense. He lifted her skirt and several moments passed in silence. The anticipation grew, and she felt that was almost worse than the spanking itself would be. Just as she was about to turn to look at him, he brought his hand down hard on her butt. It didn't hurt very much, not at first, as the padding of the diaper dampened the blows somewhat. As he continued to spank her, however, the pain grew in intensity. She began to squirm to get away, but his firm hand around her waist kept her locked in place. The pain and humiliation began to mount, and Amber kicked her legs futilely.

To make matters worse, she could feel the heat between her legs that told her that she liked what he was doing to her, despite the embarrassment and pain. Or possibly because of it. The thought only made her cry harder as shame and desire made her whole body tremble.

"You need to learn to obey Daddy," he explained calmly. He methodically covered every square inch of her bottom without mercy. The blows growing faster and harder as he went. She began to wail as the onslaught continued and she soon found herself so overwhelmed with emotion and sensation that her bladder simply released itself. It was a relief physically, but also mentally, a huge wave of satisfaction washed over her as she knew that Daddy would be pleased with her once again.

"I peed," she cried out, sobbing with relief. The spanking stopped at last, and Malcolm scooped her up into his arms, holding her close. She sank against his warm chest in relief and let the rest of her sobs peter out slowly as he held her, rocking her back and forth soothingly as she cried. All of the fear and embarrassment came flooding out of her along with her tears, along with a multitude of unidentifiable emotions that had built up over time. She let it all out, feeling completely safe and supported in his arms.

"There, isn't that better?" he murmured against her hair as he sobs began to slow down. She gripped her arms around his neck and nodded, noticing how not only did her bladder feel better, but she felt oddly cleansed after having such an intense cry. Now, with his arms around her, keeping her safe, she felt more open and free. She sighed happily, letting herself relax completely in his embrace. She even enjoyed the warm puffiness between her legs, still glowing with pride at her accomplishment. After a long time, he began to pat and squeeze the now puffy diaper. She was sure that she felt a bulge in his pants as he touched her and it was a relief to know that she wasn't the only one who had gotten turned on.

"Ready to get cleaned up, little one?" he asked. Again, she nodded, feeling a bit shy suddenly. At first, the wetness in her diaper had been warm and pleasant, but now she found herself wanting to be rid of the stickiness between her legs. He picked her up and carried her to the changing table.

"Daddy is so very proud of you, baby girl. You did such a good job of using your diaper, and you took your spanking so well. It will get easier to use your diaper, and before you know it, you'll love it, you'll see." He took the old, soggy diaper off, bundling it up and throwing it away. His praise and reassurance made her glow with pride. He began to clean her up. The baby wipe was soft and sensual against her pussy. Malcolm took his time, lovingly caressing her with the wipe, his breath obviously quickening as he did so. It was having an effect on her as well; the hungry look on his face igniting the desire that had begun to kindle when he spanked her. Again, she expected him to want to fuck her then or make some kind of move in that direction at least, but instead, he only replaced her diaper with a clean one and let her down again.

"Daddy has to get some work done in his office. Think you'll be ok on your own for a little while?"

"Yes, Daddy," she said. It was amazing to her how a single day of this lifestyle had already made her feel so regressed. She did feel a little nervous about being by herself for a while, strangely enough, but she was determined to put on a brave face for Daddy. Already, making him proud seemed like the most important thing in the world to her.

"I have some toys and coloring books for you to play with," he said, showing her the toy box and the little bookshelf with coloring books.

"Can I watch TV?" she asked hopefully, but he shook his head.

"Not now, little one. You can watch some cartoons before bed tonight if you are a good girl." She pouted slightly but nodded anyway, knowing that it would be futile to argue. Her still sore bottom reminded her to be on her best behavior. She crouched down to examine the toys more closely, her face lighting up when she discovered a race car track with a dozen or so cars to race.

"Have fun, baby girl," he said, watching her become engrossed with constructing the track for a moment before going back to his office, closing the door behind him.

Chapter 6

He came back sometime later to announce that dinner was ready. As he opened the door, the scent of chicken and herbs wafted into the room, and Amber's stomach suddenly growled. She had been so lost in her playtime that she hadn't even noticed how much time had passed or that she was hungry. Again, he fed her in the highchair, cutting her food up for her and feeding it to her one bite at a time. Already, her regression was beginning to feel normal. She was growing used to being fed and changed and had even enjoyed her playtime without feeling self-conscious about it. As he fed her, she couldn't help but wonder if those tendencies had been there all along or if her desire for him, her need to please him, was what made those activities so enjoyable for her. When they had finished eating, Malcolm cleaned up quickly and then announced that it was bath time. He carried her to the bathroom and turned on the water, sprinkling in some bubbles to make the bath nice and foamy. There were some bath time toys, rubber duckies, and plastic tugboats and the like along the rim of the tub that she looked forward to playing with.

"Arms up," he commanded and lifted her dress over her head. He took a moment to admire her semi-naked form, her smooth skin, and perky breasts. As his eyes moved over her, she could feel a familiar heat rising in her face and a tingle between her legs, the hunger in his face making her feel both flustered and aroused. "You are so beautiful, baby girl. So perfect." He took her diaper off next, tossing it in the trash, and ran his hands lightly over her skin, exploring her stomach, hips, and buttocks with his fingertips. His light touch raised goosebumps on her skin, and she could feel herself getting wet as he let his hands wander lower, grazing over her inner thighs and the outside of her sex. She gasped softly as he dipped a finger into her folds quickly, smirking as he found the wetness pooled there. He raised a finger to his lips, keeping her gaze locked with his as he tasted her juices.

"Oh, baby girl, whatever has gotten you so wet?" he teased. He stepped closer to her, placing his hands on either side of her face, kissing her lightly on the lips. She leaned in for more, but he pulled back, picking her up to lower her into the tub, which was now full of water and bubbles. He took a loofah and scrubbed her entire body lovingly and thoroughly. It felt so wonderful to be pampered. She couldn't recall the last time she had been the object of such intense focus, much less from such a handsome man. The warm water was so relaxing while his touch was both soothing and stirring. She surrendered to the sensations, letting herself go as he lavished her with attention. She was so zoned out that it almost felt like no time had passed before he was rinsing her off and draining the tub. He lifted her up and wrapped her in a towel, cradling her to his chest. He didn't seem to mind that she was getting his shirt wet with her still dripping wet hair. He sat on the rim of the tub and held her for a long time, kissing the top of her head as she slowly dripped dry. He held her so tightly that she found it hard to believe that she had only known this man for a little more than a day. He certainly seemed to be a man of great passion and deep emotion, based on the time they had spent together so far. She had been expecting a great deal of kinky sex, but cuddles and loving bubble baths were a surprise.

A very welcome surprise, she thought, burrowing her face further into his chest. It may have been a surprise, but it turned out to be exactly what she needed. Eventually, he rose and carried her to her nursery, laying her down on the crib. He brought out a pink frilly nightgown from the dresser and a fresh diaper. After he had dressed her, he began combing out her hair, delicately unsnarling the knots.

"So, after a full day of living here, what do you think? Would you like to continue?" he asked, his voice low and velvety. It was the first time he had spoken to her as an adult all day, and she found it was a bit difficult to shift gears and it took her a moment to find her words.

"Yes, Daddy," she said. "It isn't exactly what I expected, but I like it here." He smiled and patted her head. He looked so nice when he smiled, she noticed.

"Let me guess, you thought we would be fucking by now?" he teased. She found herself blushing but nodded, admitting that it was true. "Not to brag, but if it were just about sex, I wouldn't need to hire someone. You are here to fulfill all of my needs, little one, and that goes far beyond just the simple act of intercourse. We will get around to that when the time is right, of course. In the meantime, I have a need to nurture, to protect. I need someone in my life who belongs to me completely, who will give me not only their body but their obedience as well. Being a Daddy is just who I am, and I can't keep that confined to just the bedroom. That's why I enter into these arrangements. Does that make a little more sense, baby girl?" She nodded and smiled at him, happy to have that little glimpse into his inner thoughts.

"Now, that's enough grown-up talk. Ready for bed, little one?" She rubbed her eyes, feeling a bit tired but not ready to end the day yet.

"Almost," she said. He laughed and took the hint.

"Alright, I will read you one book before bedtime. Deal?"

"Deal!" she said gleefully. He tucked her in and brought her a selection of stuffies to sleep with. Before it was all said and done, he ended up reading her two and a half books before she nodded off to sleep. They were relatively short books, appropriate for her regressed state of mind, and her excitement kept her from drifting off. Finally, her breaths grew long and even, and he let himself out as quietly as possible.

Chapter 7

Malcolm closed the door behind him, letting out a huge breath that he didn't realize that he had been holding. As he walked the short distance down the hall to his bedroom, he began to chide himself for his foolish behavior. In every contract that he had ever signed with a little, he had always included one important rule: do not fall in love. But for some reason, when he was writing up the contract with Amber, he couldn't bring himself to include it this time. He couldn't place what it was exactly; after all, they had only met for that initial interview at the time that he was drawing it up. Even then, he could already tell there was something special about her, some little voice in his head telling him that if he put in that clause, he would live to regret it. As he spent the day with her, he began to be able to pinpoint what it was that had him so ensorcelled. She was sweet, naturally submissive and eager to please. Contrastingly, she also seemed to have a dirty side to her that responded well to his dominance over her. The combination was intoxicating, and he feared that he was in danger of falling for this one.

Would that be such a bad thing, he found himself wondering. The bachelor lifestyle was beginning to lose its charms. He had to admit. For so long, he had told himself that he didn't have time for the complications of romance. There was nothing complicated about the way Amber made him feel, however. She was a joy to be around, and he could already feel his disposition improving after one day with her. It felt good to have someone to take care of again, especially someone so sweet. He quickly pushed the thought out of his head, telling himself that he was getting all excited over nothing. They had only just met, no need to get himself all worked up over something that could potentially fizzle out within the week. Just in case it didn't, he did have to admit that he was glad that he had left out the love clause. If she did stick around, there was no way he would be able to adhere to it. Still, she had a grip over his thoughts as few women ever had before. He thought about her sexy body and how cute and innocent she looked when she was only wearing her diaper. He thought about how wet her pussy had gotten just from being naked in front of him, how the very act of making him happy seemed to turn her on. It was his preference not to have sex with his submissives until he was satisfied with their regression and submission to him in every way, but he could tell already that this one was going to be a challenge.

He stripped all of his clothes off and fell back on the bed, already stroking his hard cock before his head hit the pillow. Thoughts of Amber haunted him, and it was all the more painful because she was only a couple of doors away. Worse still, he knew that she was every bit as hungry for him as he was for her. He thought of sneaking into her room while she slept and climbing into bed with her, stopping her sleepy questions with a deep kiss. He longed to rip all of her clothing off and plunge himself into her, to feel her tight pussy gripping him. He imagined her moaning and thrashing with pleasure underneath him, her legs wrapped around him with all of her fierce little strength. He saw himself ramming into her without mercy, making sure that she felt how badly he wanted her with every thrust. All of the sexual tension that had been building came rushing out of him as he imagined what that would feel like and he found himself climaxing much sooner than he usually did. As he came, he imagined filling her tight pussy up with his seed, and he shuddered with ecstasy at the thought, wanting so much to feel it dripping out around him. Once he regained his breath, he began to clean himself up. It was going to be difficult to hold back, but he told himself that the waiting would make it all the sweeter once he finally gave in and claimed her. He wasn't willing to spoil the whole thing by rushing it. She was too special. No, he would wait until the time was right, no matter how many times he had to jerk himself off between then and now.

***

A few days later, Amber was deep into her regression. Malcolm praised her often, saying he was extremely happy with the progress that she had made, and it was true. She had taken to it like a natural, and it did his heart good to watch her become more playful and innocent with every passing day. She was using her diaper without hesitation, now, and depended on him for nearly everything. She looked to him to feed her, bathe her, and entertain her. Just as he had suspected from the beginning, she was the perfect submissive, and her every thought now revolved around pleasing him. It wasn't long before he decided that she was ready. She was his now, truly and completely. It was time to take their arrangement to the next level. He began by letting her dress in "big girl" clothes and letting her decide whether or not she felt like being diapered at any given time. He made it clear that it was her decision, but if she decided that she was in big girl mode within the apartment, she was to only wear skirts with no panties and no bra. Outside of the apartment, she could wear whatever she liked. That adjustment took a few days in and on itself as she experienced some mild anxiety around choosing how big or little she felt like being each day. He guided her through that phase with warmth and patience, assuring her that it was natural.

"You just need to get used to listening to your inner voice," he advised. "Most people never learn how to do that, not really, but it's a very important thing to master if you are going to be in a power exchange relationship." She bit her lip and nodded along, trying not to get too excited at the use of the word "relationship," telling herself that surely he meant it in a more general sense. They had never talked about it explicitly, but she was under the assumption that that sort of thing was off the table. The longer they spent together, the stronger her feelings for him grew into something stronger than boss/employee dynamic, even for such an unusual one as this. She kept these feelings to herself, however, not wanting to rock the boat lest he cancel the whole arrangement on the spot. She would rather have part of him than none of him, she decided.

Once she felt more comfortable with that phase, he began giving her more responsibilities, showing her the sort of tasks she would be completing as his personal assistant. At first, he only had her performing the tasks which would keep her inside, not wanting to overwhelm her with having to navigate the neighborhood and deal with strangers on top of all the other changes he was throwing at her. One thing at a time, he had insisted, and she was glad for it. Those things did sound awfully intimidating in her current state of mind.

"We'll start with my laundry," he said. "You will be responsible for washing, drying, ironing, and putting away my clothes." He explained the washer and dryer to her as she listened and nodded along as though she hadn't been doing laundry for her entire life. Something about the way that he explained everything to her as though she were just learning about it for the first time made her feel strangely turned on, and she suspected that he was doing it for similar reasons. He also made sure that she understood which fabrics could be machine washed, which had to be dry cleaned as well as which temperature and wash setting was appropriate for every item of clothing. Once he felt she was fully briefed, he gathered up the items he wanted her to attend to first.

"One more thing," he said with a twinkle in his eye. "You'll be wearing this." In his hand was a ball gag, which he held out to her. "Open," he said and placed it in her mouth, fastening it in place. She closed her lips around it, trying to find a comfortable way to hold it in her mouth. He stood back and admired the way she looked in the purple tank top and black skirt she had picked out for herself that morning, the black gag stood out in stark contrast to the cute outfit.

"There,' he said with a smile. "Now, you're perfect." He watched her as she moved around the laundry room, starting a new load of washing before tackling the pile of ironing. Something about the way that his eyes tracked her every movement told her that he loved to see her this way, attending to his needs. As she tried to accommodate the ball gag in her mouth, she found it hard to swallow. Try as she might try to contain it, drool was soon dripping down her chin and onto her pretty top. At first, she was embarrassed, thinking that surely he would think she was gross for drooling all over herself, but instead, he seemed to be rather turned on by it.

"Mmm, you look so sexy. Daddy's slutty little baby." The demeaning words only made her horny and proud, especially when he said it in such a sultry way. She stopped trying to hold it back, letting her spit fall freely down the front of her shirt. It made her tank top stick to her nipples in a rather alluring way, and she suddenly felt sexy again. Malcolm casually pulled his hard cock out as she began to iron his shirts. She froze when she saw it, her eyes bulging out wildly at the size of it. It was by far the biggest cock she had ever seen in person, and she was at once intimidated and aroused by it. On the one hand, she wasn't sure she had what it took to service a member that large but on the other hand, she wanted nothing more than to try.

"I didn't tell you to stop, did I little one?" he asked, his voice taking on a stern tone. She snapped out of her reverie, dutifully turning her attention back to his work shirts. She sprayed more starch and brought the iron down on the garment, all the time painfully aware that he was watching her and pleasuring himself. She longed to be the one to give him pleasure or at the very least, to be allowed to watch, but she was afraid that if she took her eyes away from the task at hand, she would burn his shirt. He continued to stroke himself as he watched her iron all of his shirts until they were perfect and crisp. Once that last one had been hung up, she stood before him, awaiting her next instructions.

"Come here," he said, his voice thick and raspy with lust. She complied, allowing herself to peek at his throbbing cock as she crossed the short distance between them. "Kneel." She knelt before him, hoping that he would remove her ballgag and allow her to suck on his thick, yummy cock. Or at the very least, give him a handjob. Anything to be of use to him.

"Look at me," he said. As their eyes met, he began to stroke his cock faster, frantically working himself to a climax. "Do you want to suck Daddy's cock, baby?" She nodded and made a desperate noise of affirmation. She did her best to convey to him with her eyes how much she wanted to taste him, to feel his hot cum shooting down her throat. He stroked her cheek with his free hand, and hope leaped up in her chest. To her dismay, however, he shook his head.

"You haven't earned that privilege yet, I'm afraid. Be a good girl and let Daddy cum on your face, and I'll consider letting you suck me off next time." She nodded eagerly, thrilled to be allowed to serve him in any way she could. He gripped her face harder as he neared his climax. It felt so strangely possessive, and her body thrilled at the contact. He slid his hand down and scooped up some of the drool that was hanging from her chin and used it to make his cock slick enough to stroke it faster. With a loud grunt, he sprayed his cum all over her face and tank top, soaking it further. Strangely, kneeling on the floor covered in spit and cum was the sexiest she had ever felt in her life. If someone had told her just a few weeks ago that she would be begging for some guy to cum all over her face, to be truly desperate for it, she would have laughed in their face. In just a short time she had transformed from a shy, inexperienced girl to a wanton, shameless slut. Even the thought of being a slut made her pussy ached. She longed for Malcolm to fuck her at last, but, as he said, she still had not earned that privilege. She vowed to do whatever it took to earn his cock. She would do anything if it meant relieving this terrible ache she had for him.

"Oh sweetheart, you look so sexy right now," he said, zipping his cock back into his pants. Indeed, she did feel sexy. His cum on her face seemed to mark her as his, and she wore it with pride. "Go clean yourself up, pumpkin. You can play in your room while Daddy gets dinner ready. No TV." She got up and skipped up to her room. Once she closed the door, she decided not to remove the ball gag or clean the cum off of her face right away. With a glance at the closed door, she slipped her hand under her skirt to find that her pussy was soaking wet. She touched her fingers to her face and scooped up a bit of his jizz and rubbed it over her clit. The sensation made her whole body shiver with fierce pleasure. She plunged her finger into her hungry pussy, fucking herself hard and fast. In her mind, she replayed what had just happened, how she had happily given her body up as a cum rag. She recalled him calling her a dumb baby, and the memory made her cum instantly. As waves of release washed over her, she moaned softly against the ball gag. Downstairs, Malcolm listened on the baby monitor as his baby girl made herself cum. She thought she was being quiet, but he heard every grunt and moan. He grinned at the knowledge that being used by him in such a degrading manner had made her so horny that she had to rush off and make herself cum immediately. From the sound of it, she hadn't even cleaned herself off first. He was so proud of her that he didn't even mind that she was touching herself without his permission. He idly rubbed his chin and decided that she was ready at last. He had her exactly where he wanted her.

Chapter 8

"Get ready, baby girl. We're going on a date," he announced the next afternoon. She had just woken up from her nap, and she was feeling a bit groggy, but the prospect of a date perked her right up.

"Really?!" She was so excited that she was practically squealing. It had been a couple of weeks since she had left the apartment. Maybe longer, it was hard to keep track when your days were filled with diaper changes and laundry duty. The prospect of getting to dress up and have some stimulating conversation thrilled her to the core.

"Yes, my dear. We'll be going to dinner and then to a movie. Would you like that?" Her response was to jump up and down, clapping her hands with joy. He laughed and looked at her with warm affection. Her innocence remained his favorite part about her.

"Good. Now go get ready, little one." He leaned in and whispered in her ear, his hot breath sending goosebumps all down her arms. "And make sure you shave every inch of your lovely body." Her pussy instantly flooded with desire, and she grinned at the implication. Would tonight be the night? Would the long wait finally be over?

"Yes, Daddy," she whispered in response. She scurried upstairs, her mind racing as she thought about which outfit she would wear and how she would do her hair and makeup. It had been such a long time since she had been on a date and this one was especially important to her, and she wanted to look especially nice.

If he wants to take me out, get to know me better, perhaps there is something more going on here, she dared to hope. He had a hold on her, unlike any man she had ever met before. All other men that she had dated before now seemed like boys in comparison to Malcolm. Although the logical, sensible part of her brain warned her that it was not a good idea, Amber knew that she was falling for him. She didn't know what a girl like her could offer a man like him except for her complete devotion. Everything would have to be perfect tonight. She took extra special care as she was getting ready. Not only did she shave herself completely bare, but she also did a full-body sugar scrub to get her skin as silky smooth as possible. She followed that up with a creamy lotion, getting herself so soft to the touch that even she couldn't stop running her hands over herself. Next, she styled her hair, carefully curling it and spraying it to perfection. She let it drape over shoulders, wanting to show off a more elegant side of herself this evening. She spent longer than usual on her makeup as well, even looking up a few tutorials online to make sure that she looked absolutely perfect for Malcolm. She had a feeling that he was used to a certain level of elegance in his women. For her clothes, she chose a simple low-cut black dress that hugged her curves perfectly. After some consideration, she decided that the only thing she would wear underneath was a pair of black silk thigh highs. As she studied herself in the mirror, she had to admit that she looked stunning. Her nipples stood at attention already, advertising the fact that she was braless, and she loved the feeling of the satiny material against her bare skin, thrilled with the knowledge that she was accessible to Malcolm at any moment should he choose to take her this evening. She hoped with all her heart that he would. All of this waiting was exquisite torture, but she longed to belong to him truly and completely. The last step was a pair of high heeled shoes. Amber stepped into them, grateful that she had taken the time to practice walking in them prior to wearing them out in public. They were a bit higher than she was used to but they looked so perfect with the rest of her outfit that she was happy to tolerate the slight discomfort. She was sure to grow used to them as the evening wore on.

At last, her outfit was complete, and she was ready. She practically floated down the stairs. Her excitement made her feel as light as a feather. Malcolm was waiting for her on the loveseat by the stairs, patiently flipping through a magazine. When he looked up at her, his face lit up so much that her heart did a little somersault in her chest. He looked incredible, as well, wearing a black suit so perfectly tailored that it hugged his toned figure as though it were made for him.

"Oh, little one," he breathed. "You look so beautiful. Come here let me look at you." She sauntered over to him, delighting in the way his eyes followed her every movement. As she twirled around slowly to let him see her from every angle, his eyes began to take on a hungry quality. He wrapped his hands around her waist, pulling her close to him. She felt her breath catch as she melted into his arms. He ran his hands over the silky fabric and pressed his forehead to hers. His hands traveled up her ribcage and brushed over her breasts, then up her neck and into her hair.

At last, he pulled her in for a kiss, soft and deep. It was tentative at first, almost shy, but then his tongue was pushing into her mouth, demanding to taste her. She wrapped her arms around his neck, clinging to him as he explored her mouth. Their tongues danced together, and she found herself almost swooning with pleasure as he kissed her with a building passion. Suddenly, he broke off the kiss, leaving her stunned and breathless. He grinned down at her, and she found herself thinking that when she agreed to be tortured by him, this wasn't exactly what she had in mind.

"Hungry?" he asked cheerily and held his arm out for her to take. She was too dazed even to pout so she took his arm and let him lead her to the elevator. As they descended, he let his hand rest on the curve of her ass, and the casual possessiveness made her feel weak in the knees. A town car was waiting for them outside, and Malcolm held the door open for her to get in first. She slid into the back seat, excited at the chance to see how the other half lived. She had lived in the city for a couple of years now but had never really gotten the time or the money needed to really see the sights. Even dinner and a movie sounded thrilling to her after spending the last couple of years so focused on finding her big break. Not to mention, having a driver seemed like the height of luxury to her after splitting cabs or walking everywhere. As he slid in next to her, he wrapped his arm around her shoulders. She leaned her head against him, savoring his warmth and strength. She felt safer with him than she had with any other person save her parents. Deep down, she trusted him completely and knew that he would never let anything bad happen to her as long as he was around. They didn't talk much on the way to the restaurant but rather communicated silently with caresses and sighs. He ran his fingers over her knee and up her thigh, teasing her but never going as high up as she would have wanted. By the time they reached their destination, she was squirming in her seat, and her wetness was coating the inside of her legs. All she wanted was for him to fuck her right then and there in the car, but she knew that he was enjoying making her wait.

The restaurant was very upscale, and Amber felt a bit out of place. Luckily, Malcolm took the lead, indicating to her where to sit and helping her to navigate the French menu. He requested a secluded table in the corner where once seated, they were completely out of view of the rest of the restaurant thanks to some large potted plants and a strategically placed column, and it almost felt as though they were alone. When the waiter came by, Malcolm ordered drinks and hors d'oeuvres, and she let herself relax and enjoy the ambiance. It felt nice to relax and let someone else take care of the details. Malcolm ordered a bottle of champagne for the two of them to split.

"Now, show Daddy your pretty pink pussy," he said as soon as the waiter was out of earshot. Amber blushed and looked around nervously, but her knees were already parting. Her body responded to his command as though it were the most natural thing in the world. She lifted up the hem of her dress, exposing her freshly shaved pussy as he took her in with hungry eyes.

"Good girl," he smirked. "Now, touch yourself." This time, she hesitated. Surely the waiter would be back with their champagne at any moment. Sensing her reluctance, he leaned forward and gave her a stern look.

"Don't you want to be a good girl for Daddy?" She gulped and nodded, needing his approval more than anything. "Then do as I say and touch yourself." She took in a deep breath, steeled her resolve, and slid a finger up her smooth slit, already dewey with lust. It felt so nice as she twirled her finger around her tender button, Malcolm's eyes glued to her glistening folds, that she completely forgot that they were in public. That is until the waiter returned with their champagne. Amber let out an involuntary "eep" and pulled the hem of her dress down. She turned a deeper shade of red and did her best to avoid the gaze of the waiter, who quickly put their drinks down and left.

"Did I tell you you could stop?" he asked, his

voice carrying the unspoken threat of hard spankings.

"No, Daddy." She lifted her dress once more, fingers resuming their exploration of her private parts.

"Why do you look so embarrassed, little one? You're Daddy's little slave, and you don't care who knows it. Say it." She met his gaze shyly and did as he commanded.

"I'm Daddy's little slave, and I don't care who knows it." As the words came out of her mouth, she could feel her pussy get wetter. Being under his control was so intoxicating.

"Let Daddy taste how dripping wet you are." She reached out her fingers, slick with her juices, and he captured them in his mouth. As he tasted her, his lips curled into a seductive smile, and he made a satisfied "mmm." The sound made a subtle vibration on her fingertips, making her giggle a little.

"Good girl," he said, returning her hand to her lap. "Now drink your champagne." They toasted to a successful partnership, and the bubbles tickled Amber's nose as she drank.

"So," he said, putting his glass down again. "Tell me more about yourself, Amber. Tell me about your history." She almost giggled at the word "history" and the implication it carried that she had some grand story to tell. She told him about growing up in a quiet, small-town, always doing well in school, never one to get in trouble or rebel in any way. Then she told him about how she left home a few years back to pursue her dream of acting. He seemed surprised when she mentioned that last part.

"You've never mentioned that before," he said, leaning forward, his gaze suddenly shifting from curious to penetrating.

"Why not?"

"Well, it's on hold right now, obviously. I couldn't possibly have enough time to audition and do my job properly." He shook his head, hissing under his breath.

"No, that won't do at all," he said. "From

now on, auditioning for parts is now officially part of your work duties." For a moment, she was so stunned that she didn't know what to say.

"Really? Why would you want that?" It didn't really make sense to her why he would want her to do something that would interfere with her being available to him twenty-four-seven, something that he had made clear was very important to him.

"Because one of the main duties of a Daddy is making sure that his little is happy. It's my job to make sure that all of your needs are met, including your creative needs and your life goals. If acting is important to you then it's important to me too. Tomorrow, I expect you to start looking for casting calls, and I want a daily report on your progress." She blushed, feeling like the luckiest girl in the world. If she thought it was hard not to fall for him before, it was going to be next to impossible if he kept this up. She reached across the table and squeezed his hand.

"Thank you, Daddy," was all that she could

manage to say, she was so overwhelmed with emotion. She could only hope that her eyes and the touch of her hand could convey her gratitude better than her words. Hopefully, he would let her show him her gratitude in a more tangible way later in the evening.

"Of course, princess. If you tell me who you are going to be auditioning with, I'll put in a good word for you. I know a few people in show business." That made her frown.

"I'd rather you didn't do that. I'd rather get the part on my own merits." He raised an eyebrow at that but didn't seem to be angry.

"Integrity move, baby girl. I have to say I'm impressed by that. Not many people would pass up a chance to get an inside track to success." She shrugged, somewhat embarrassed by the compliment.

"I don't know that it's an integrity move per se. I just feel like I will enjoy my success more if its a result of my own talent and hard work." He smiled at that and shook his head in a bemused fashion.

"I think that says more about your integrity than you realize. But if you don't want me to interfere, then I won't. I still expect daily progress reports, however. And I assume that helping you to memorize your lines is considered an appropriate form of support?" She giggled with delight.

"I would love that!" He actually looked happy at the thought of helping her, and the sight of it made her heart melt. She knew then that it didn't really matter what his intentions were, she was already falling in love with him, and there was nothing she could do about it. It was already too late. He ordered their entrees and spent the rest of the meal filling her in on his past. He, too, was from a small town which she found surprising given his polished, cosmopolitan air. He had gotten into school on a scholarship and decided to go to law school to become a public defender. After doing that for a few years, he said that he felt drained and underappreciated. It was around then that he was approached by a private law firm who was impressed by his record. Due to his burnout, he agreed to come on as a consultant provided he was allowed to work from home most of the time.

"I found that I needed to seclude myself from humanity from a while after dealing with the worst of the worst for so long. I'm feeling much better these days. If I'm honest, my only reason for still working from home is that I'm spoiled. I just got used to it, and now I don't want to go back." They shared a laugh and then began to contemplate dessert. Amber was considering a chocolate cake that sounded particularly divine but wasn't sure she wanted to indulge. Malcolm shamelessly encouraged her to go for it.

"Why would you deny yourself the pleasure when it is so very delicious?" he asked, winking suggestively. She immediately felt her core clench with desire and wondered how he could manage to make her heart race with just a wink.

"Well, when you put it like that," she giggled, blushing ever so slightly. He ordered a slice for them to share, and she was very glad that he did because it was every bit as delicious as it had sounded. Even as she grew uncomfortably full, she still felt like it was worth every bite. As they left, she noticed that he left the waiter an especially large tip and she hoped that it would help to make up for anything he may or may not have seen.

Chapter 9

Even the movie theater he took her too was upscale compared to what she was used to, stadium seating, and a huge IMAX screen. On the few occasions when she ventured out to the movies, it was always to the dollar theater. Malcolm insisted that they sit in the back and as the lights went down, she began to see why. He lifted the armrest that was between them and started caressing her knee, slowly making his way up her thigh. Her breath quickened, and her eyes darted around the sparsely populated theater. No one was sitting near them, and there was no reason why anyone should notice that he was getting handsy as long as she managed to keep quiet. She opened her legs wider, giving him access to her hungry pussy. As his fingers brushed against her folds, it was harder to suppress a cry of pleasure than she had imagined. His fingers explored her wetness, seeking out her already swollen clit. She bit her lip to hold back the wanton moan that wanted to escape as he teased her lightly.

"Does that feel good, princess?" he teased, murmuring quietly in her ear. She could only nod and grip the armrest on the other side of her to try to maintain her composure. As good as it felt, she longed to have his fingers inside of her, or better yet, his cock, the light pressure on her clit not nearly enough to ease her ache. If anything, it was making it worse.

"What's that?" he prompted. "I couldn't hear you over the movie." As he spoke, he continued to stimulate her, driving her wild with pleasure. It was taking all of her mental energy not to cry out in ecstasy and blow their cover. She burned with embarrassment as she imagined being thrown out of the theater for lewd acts. When she didn't answer right away, he fisted his hand into her hair, pulling it hard enough to force her head back. He leaned in and whispered in her ear, his tone growing impatient.

"I asked you a question, little girl. If you don't answer me, you will regret it when we get back home." She clenched her eyes closed, shutting out everything else in an effort to concentrate.

"Yes, Daddy," she managed to whisper. "That feels so good."

"Good," he growled and tightened his grip on her hair. She gasped, but the music playing under the action scene drowned it out. "Is this what you've been craving, little one?"

"Yes, Daddy," she whimpered. His finger began to travel down, teasing her entrance. She shivered in anticipation, but he didn't give her what she craved, not yet. She was beginning to wonder if she would ever get satisfaction.

"You're so wet, pumpkin. I bet that's not all you've been craving. Why don't you tell Daddy all about it?" She took a deep breath and opened her eyes, peeking to see if anyone had noticed their naughty little game. Everyone seemed fixated on the movie, and so she focused her concentration on answering him.

"I've been craving your cock," she whispered, grateful that no one could see her blush.

"What else?" he hissed in her ear.

"Fucking you. I want to fuck you so bad, Daddy." By now, she was such a horny, dripping mess that she didn't care who saw or heard. All that mattered was the finger between her legs and the heaven it promised.

"I know you have. Look at you. You're just a squirming, whimpering little slut so desperate for her Daddy's cock that she'll let him finger her in public. Isn't that right?" His teasing words only made her situation worse, made her pussy ache for him.

"Yes, Daddy. Please finger my desperate little cunt." With a growl of approval, he plunged his finger in at last, and she took it all, struggling not to scream out with satisfaction. As he finger fucked her, it felt so amazing that she had to clamp her hand down over her mouth to muffle the soft noises of pleasure that she couldn't hold back. With every thrust, she saw stars behind her closed eyes and felt herself building quickly to a climax.

"You're not about to cum already, are you pumpkin? Right here in front of all of these people? Are you really that much of greedy little slut? How cute." She couldn't hold it back anymore. She gripped the armrest as powerful waves of ecstasy washed over her. Somehow, she managed not to make a sound louder than a whimper as she came. When her body relaxed once again, Malcolm finally let go of the grip he had on her hair and pulled her to him for a kiss. Her breath was still shaky, but it soon stilled again as their tongues met over and over. The kiss grew deeper as though he couldn't get enough of her. His hands began to wander over her thighs, up her hips and waist, seeking out her breasts. He tweaked her nipples beneath the thin material of the dress, making them stand at attention. Already, she could feel the heat building between her legs again, her desire for him far from sated. As their making outreached a frenzied state, the credits began to roll on the movie. Amber dimly thought that she didn't see a single second of the film and had no idea what it was even about. Malcolm took her by the hand and began to lead her toward the exit.

"Come one, kitten. Let's get you home and in Daddy's bed."

Chapter 10

He couldn't keep his hands off of her in the car, raising the partition between them and the driver so that he could freely explore her body, kissing her neck and breasts. She moaned and gripped his broad shoulders, wishing that the driver would go faster so that they could be back in their little love nest. He couldn't stop kissing her in the elevator either, devouring her with all of the passion that had built up between them over the past few weeks. As soon as the elevator doors opened, he picked her up and carried her over the threshold, up the stairs, and directly to his bedroom. She had never been in his room before but didn't really get a chance to admire it as they tumbled onto the bed together, already pulling off one another's clothes. He tugged at her dress so impatiently that it ripped.

"I'll buy you another one," he growled as if she could give a shit about the dress. Luckily, she didn't have anything on underneath for him to ruin in his haste. She was more careful with his jacket and shirt and only got his shirt halfway unbuttoned before he ripped that off as well, sending buttons flying. She had a sneaking suspicion that she would be tasked with sewing those back on once they had cooled down. He settled his weight down on top of her, spreading her legs with his knee. For a moment, he only studied her closely as though trying to memorize her face, stroking her cheek with his thumb. She was mesmerized by his gaze, even as her body burned for more.

"You're mine, completely mine. Say it."

"I'm completely yours." As she said it, she realized how deeply she meant it. She had given her heart and mind to him, and now it was time to give her body as well. He sighed and kissed her with a tenderness that surprised her. Slowly, the kiss deepened once more, and she could feel his erection pressing into her. She fumbled with his belt but didn't make any progress. Finally, he took over, removing his pants and underwear, kicking them off to the side. At the sight of his large member, a small shiver of anticipation went through her. The moment that she had been dreaming of was finally here. He was hers. She reverently ran her hands over his well-muscled figure. His body was like a work of art, and she was so grateful to at last have the chance to touch him. He, too, ran his hands over her body, seeming to know instinctively all of her pleasure points. He began to rub his hard cock over her slick folds, making her cry out with pleasure and an aching desire for more.

"Oh, baby girl. You're so beautiful." As he ran the tip of his cock over her clit, she dug her nails into his back. Her earlier orgasm only made her more sensitive, and having his cock, so close was driving her wild. He kissed her neck tenderly, not seeming to notice her impatience to have him inside of her. He seemed to prefer to take his time and savor her instead. She ran her hands down his brawny back and to his firm buttocks, pulling him closer to her. She had savored him more than enough, she felt, now she needed to get fucked.

"You want Daddy's cock that bad, little one?" he teased and then nibbled her earlobe, sending a jolt of electric pleasure throughout her body. She moaned loudly and moved her hips, seeking to find the angle which would allow him access.

"I want your cock so bad," she moaned, too horny to care if she sounded desperate. She was desperate, desperate to have him at last. "Please fuck me, Daddy. I need you." His only response was a happy sigh before he plunged himself inside of her at last. She cried out with relief and delight as his thick cock stretched her open, filling her up more completely than anyone ever had before. His girth was so large that it was slightly uncomfortable, but she found that the mild pain only heightened her pleasure. She opened her legs wider, wanting to take him deeper inside of her, wanting to feel every inch of him. It felt so good to be claimed by him at last, and every thrust felt like an affirmation that she belonged to him.

"Fuck, you feel so good," he growled, driving into her harder. "You're so perfect." She was too lost in her own pleasure to respond with anything other than a loud moan. She bucked her hips upward to meet his, every thrust bringing her closer to another orgasm. Never before had anyone fucked her so passionately, and it was driving her to heights of pleasure that she didn't even know existed.

"You're so tight, little one. Are you going to cum for Daddy again?" His voice with thick with lust and something else, amusement perhaps. He slowed to an agonizingly slow pace, and she could feel her needy pussy pulsing around him, crying out for the climax that had been rapidly approaching. He grinned down at her, clearly enjoying torturing her. She groaned and gripped his buttocks, trying to coax him back into the fast and hard rhythm that she craved so badly.

"Please, Daddy. Please ..." she cried but to no avail. His slow movements felt wonderful but were not what she needed. What she needed was that hard pounding rhythm, the dominant insistence that she submit to the pleasure he desired her to have.

"Poor greedy little slut," he teased, prolonging her torture. "You're already begging for Daddy to let you cum, aren't you?"

"Y-yes, please! Please let me cum, Daddy." He was done teasing her. He pounded into her with such force that she immediately came undone beneath him. Her fingers clawed at the air, and she felt for a moment that she might lose her mind. Her body shook with waves of pleasure so intense that she couldn't even form a sound. She could only grip him with her thighs until the waves stopped.

"Oh princess," he whispered as she collapsed against the mattress, her limbs feeling like they had turned to jelly. He once again slowed down his pace and captured her lips with his with a shaky sigh. She melted open for him, feeling more sated and more complete than she ever had before. He cupped her face with his hands, slowly but steadily pumping into her as they kissed. "You're such a good girl. My perfect girl." Suddenly, he pulled out of her, deftly flipping her over onto her stomach. He pulled her hips up and plunged into her once again. The change of position seemed to make her body come alive with the new sensations. His thick cock stretched her open and seemed to hit all the right spots every time he hammered into her. She gripped the pillows, holding on as he rutted into her like a frenzied animal. He no longer seemed to care about savoring it. He grabbed a fistful of her hair, and she felt so owned by him, so used in a deliciously sexy way. No longer did he seem to care about her pleasure. She was there to service him, to service his cock and it filled her with a deep sense of pride. At last, she could feel his cock swelling inside of her, and she knew that she was about to receive her reward finally. With a loud groan, he unloaded himself, pumping her full of his hot seed, the sensation making her toes curl. He collapsed his weight against her, and together, they fell onto the mattress in a sweaty, panting heap. They lay like that for several minutes, both of them completely satisfied and too spent to move. Eventually, he rolled off of her and pulled her to him, wrapping her tightly in his arms. They kissed, no less passionately now that they had had their fill of one another than they had before. If anything, she felt as though experiencing how good it could be between them only served to heighten her craving for him. When he broke off the kiss, she whimpered with disappointment. He chuckled and kissed her lightly on the forehead.

"Go to sleep, little one," he whispered into her hair. "There will be plenty of time for all of that in the morning. Get your rest, my dear." She quieted, knowing that he was right. Her body was sore and exhausted, and recharging seemed like the sensible thing to do. She willed her body to settle down, and she relaxed into his warmth. As he pulled the covers over them, she was already yawning.

"Good night, Daddy," she murmured and wrapped her arms around him as tightly as she could as though he were one of her stuffies.

"Good night, princess."

Chapter 11

When she awoke the next morning, Malcolm was already up. She heard him banging around in the kitchen and whistling a happy tune all the way from upstairs. It was a sound that filled her heart with joy. She stretched out on the luxurious linens and took a moment to bask in her own happiness. The previous night felt like a wonderful dream, except the wetness between her legs and Malcolm's cheery tune assured it that it was very real. After a bit of a lie-in, she reluctantly got out of his bed and padded to her room, still naked. She picked out her outfit for the day, opting for a very short mini skirt and a crop top, adhering to the no bra or panty rule. She washed the makeup from last off of her face and brushed her hair, then went downstairs to greet Malcolm.

"Good morning, princess." He greeted her

with a grin and a kiss on the forehead. "You are looking especially sexy this morning." He grabbed her bare ass under her skirt, squeezing it hard as he pulled her against him.

"Thank you, Daddy," she answered, her voice a little breathless from the butterflies she felt as he handled her so possessively.

"Breakfast is ready," he said with a wink. "You had better eat up. We have a very busy day ahead of us." She sat at the table on most days now, only eating in her high chair when she was feeling particularly like being coddled. He served up scrambled eggs and toast with coffee. As soon as the first bite hit her lips, she realized how ravenous she was. She was so hungry that she even had seconds. As she put her fork down, at last, she noticed that he was looking at her with an odd twinkle in his eyes.

"All done?" She nodded with a satisfied smile on her face. "Good. You're on dish duty this morning." Something about the way he looked at her when he said it made her look forward to it.

She wondered what devious plan he had cooked up.

"Yes, Daddy," she said, making her voice low and seductive. She gathered up their dirty dishes and took them to the sink. As she rinsed them off, she felt his hands encircle her waist. He pressed his already hard member against her ass, making her gasp as a desperate need to have him gripped her body.

"Don't stop, little one," he whispered in her ear. With a great deal of effort, she returned her focus to the task at hand. His hands slid under her skirt and once again squeezed her bare ass, his fingers digging into her soft flesh. She let out a soft moan and could feel herself getting wet. As he spread her cheeks open, she found it difficult to keep her concentration on the plate she was washing. That earned her a slap on the ass, making her yelp in surprise. It was a lot more painful when there was no diaper there to dampen the blow.

"I said not to stop, didn't I?" he growled.

"Sorry, Daddy," she whimpered, the mild

burning of her ass cheek only serving to make her more horny for him. He slipped his finger between her moist folds, making a noise of satisfaction at the wetness he found there. This time, she remembered to continue to wash the plate despite the jolt of pleasure coming from between her legs.

"You don't seem very sorry. You seem like a desperate little slut to me. Aren't you baby girl?" She slowly ran a sponge across the plate, using all of her concentration to focus on what she had been told to do. It wasn't enough, however, and he smacked her ass again, harder, making her hiss at the pain.

"I asked you a question, baby girl," he growled and spanked her ass one more time to drive home his point. She chided herself, not focussing harder, wishing she could be better for him.

"Yes, Daddy. I am a desperate little slut." At last, the plate was clean. She rinsed it off and put it to the side. With shaky fingers, she picked up the next one and began to clean it as well.

"Good girl," he said. "I'm glad that you know what you are. My domesticated little fuck slave." The words made her shiver with delight. She heard the sound of metal on metal and knew that he was unzipping his pants, and she longed to have him inside of her. He nestled his hard cock between her cheeks and growled into her ear.

"Say it."

"I'm your domesticated little fuck slave." Her words almost came as moans. She whimpered as he began to slide his hard cock closer to her entrance, teasing her. It was so difficult to keep her attention on washing the dishes, but she was doing her best. She finished the plate that she was working on and moved on to the pots and pans.

"That's right," he said. "You are here to serve me." With that, he pushed himself inside of her, burying himself deep within her with one thrust. She gasped as his huge cock stretched her open and nearly dropped the pot that she was cleaning. He didn't seem to notice. He was too busy pounding into her.

"Oh, sweetie," he said. "Your pussy is so tight. I love fucking you." He was fucking her so hard and so fast, clearly intent on using her body to pleasure himself. She found his control over her to be so deliciously erotic, and every thrust sent a lightning bolt of pleasure through her.

"You're Daddy's good little slut," he snarled. Suddenly, he was pulsing inside of her, grunting loudly as he came. His hot cum felt so wonderful inside of her that her eyes rolled back. He slowly pumped into her a few more times before pulling out. As his semen dripped out of her, she almost felt a sense of regret, wanting to keep him inside of her for longer. He zipped himself up, but he wasn't done with her yet.

"Finish up these dishes and report to my office when you're done," he said, giving her ass one final smack before walking away.

Chapter 12

She finished the few remaining dishes as quickly as she could. Nervously, she smoothed her hair and skirt, wondering what he had in store for her next. She left the semen that was dripping down her leg, loving how dirty it made her feel. She had a feeling that Malcolm would feel the same way. He was working at his desk when she came into his office, a coil of rope sitting on the desk next to his computer. He gestured toward the velvet settee opposite his desk, indicating that she should sit. She sat and waited several moments before he reached a stopping point with his work. She had grown accustomed to being made to wait by now. Finally, he picked up the rope and came over to where she was sitting. Without a word of explanation, he began to tie her hands behind her back. Then, he wrapped the rope around her thighs, arranging her so that her legs were forced up and open, leaving her pussy exposed for his viewing pleasure. He stepped back to his desk to retrieve two items, a small vibrator, and a ball gag. He slid the vibrator into her pussy, making her shiver and make a small noise of pleasure. She was still slick with his cum, and it slid in quite easily. It was an unusual design, curving back onto itself so that it stimulated both the g-spot and the clitoris at the same time. Lastly, he slid the ball gag over her head, fastening it into place. She was completely helpless, completely at his mercy. He could do whatever he wanted to her, and the thought made her pussy ache.

"Well, don't you look absolutely perfect. Daddy's perfect little fucktoy. Now, let's try this out." He took out his phone and tapped the screen a few times. She felt a powerful vibration between her legs, making her legs quiver. A little squeak escaped her lips from behind the ball gag as it hit both of her most sensitive areas at once. He watched her intently, letting the vibrator go on for several seconds before stopping it with a few more taps on his phone.

"You are mine, and I will play with you whenever and wherever I wish. I control that greedy little pussy of yours now. Is that understood?" **She nodded and made a noise of affirmation,** her breath quickening at the thought of being controlled by him so literally. With this little gadget, he could give or deny her pleasure at the touch of a button.

"Good girl. Now sit there and look pretty for Daddy," he said and went back to sit at his desk. She waited for what felt like an eternity, her entire body tingling in anticipation. He had aroused her desire when he fucked her earlier and sitting here with her pussy exposed, bound in place. It was only growing stronger. She began to squirm, desperate for stimulation, but still, he ignored her and continued on with his work.

At last, he stopped and turned to her again. He made no moves towards her, only stared at her for a long while, as though she were a piece of art in a museum to be studied. At last, he smirked and picked up his phone.

"I see you squirming over there, little one," he teased. "Greedy for more?" She felt the vibe come to life between her legs and made a choked cry, muffled by the ball gag. He turned the vibe off again, looking very pleased with himself. "That's the lowest setting, by the way. There are many more powerful settings than that." She shivered in anticipation, waiting for him to turn the vibe on once more. He kept her waiting, however, turning his attention back to his work. She wondered vaguely if he was even working on anything or if it was an elaborate ruse designed to drive her mad. If it was, it was working. She decided as she began to squirm again. The thought was cut short as the vibe came back, even stronger than before. She hadn't even seen him move that time, and it caught her completely off guard. Her muscles tensed as the strong sensation had her immediately on the verge of an orgasm. She was all too aware that he hadn't given her permission to cum, however, and she held herself back somehow. Just as she thought she couldn't hold back any longer, he suddenly turned the vibe off again. She sat there panting, her pussy clenching around the vibe, seeking the orgasm it had been denied.

"You look so cute like that," he sneered. "Legs wide open like the greedy slut you are, unable to hide how desperately horny you are. I know you want to cum, don't you, princess?" She nodded, pleading with him with her eyes. She wanted to cum more than anything in the world. The vibe came back to life, and Amber couldn't even think as her orgasm came roaring back. Her body tensed up, trying desperately to keep from cumming without permission. As he turned it off again, she relaxed against the settee, panting and sweaty.

"You didn't cum, did you little one?" he growled, and she shook head. Despite how desperately she wanted to, she was still his obedient little fuck-slave, and she would hold off as long as she could.

"Good girl," he purred. "That's Daddy pussy, his toy. Isn't that right?" She couldn't even nod as he turned the vibe up yet another level. She made wild, keening noises, wordlessly begging him to allow her to release. He turned it off again and unzipped his pants, taking out his hard cock. He stroked himself as he watched her, breathlessly squirming on the settee. He watched her for so long. She wondered if he was going to jerk himself off, leaving her unsatisfied yet again. She couldn't even see his cock from where he sat, denied even the satisfaction of watching him pleasure himself. Finally, he stood, cock in hand, and came over to where she sat. He removed the ball gag and slid his cock past her lips, groaning with satisfaction as she swallowed his swollen member. He tapped his phone, bringing the vibe on again.

"I know you want to cum, baby girl. Luckily for you, I'm very pleased with your behavior so far today. You can cum as many times as you want as you deepthroat Daddy. Go on, let it out." He turned up the intensity as he spoke, simultaneously pushing himself further and further down her throat. She couldn't hold it in anymore. As her climax shook her body, her eyes rolled back in her head. He kept right on fucking her throat, growling with satisfaction as her body convulsed with ecstasy. She was so lost in her orgasm that his thick cock slid effortlessly down her throat.

"There, isn't that better, kitten?" he taunted, pulling his cock out long enough for her to catch her breath. She couldn't respond, however, as the vibe was still going strong, sending aftershocks rippling all through her body. Her first orgasm had barely finished when a second one came crashing over her, and he pushed himself back down her throat as she came, wanting her to associate having his cock down her throat with the powerful orgasm that ripped through her body. He gripped the back of her head, pulling her further onto his shaft as she choked and whimpered around him. She fought to take his girth down her throat, loving the way it made her feel, how it only added to the heavenly sensations between her legs. Just when she thought she might lose her mind from the pleasure, he turned the vibe back off. He didn't stop fucking her throat, however, grunting as her eyes rolled back in her head, and she felt her mind go completely blank. She was just a vessel for his pleasure now, capable only of doing what she was told. He looked down at her with a smirk, knowing that she was deep in subspace by now. He turned the vibe back on as high as it would go, curious how many times he could make her cum. As her eyes fluttered closed, he changed the setting again, making the vibe pulse on and off in an undulating pattern. She found the change of stimulation to be even more arousing and she enthusiastically bobbed her head up and down on his cock, surrendering to him completely. He turned the vibe up to the third level, this time at a strong and steady pulse. She could feel yet another orgasm building and knew it wouldn't be long before it came crashing over her. Just for fun, he cut the vibe off just as she was on the edge of cumming. She whimpered with disappointment and squirmed, trying desperately to stimulate her aching pussy.

"Poor, cum drunk little slut," he laughed, stroking her cheek adoringly. "You've already cum so many times, and you still want more."

"Yes, please," she murmured, her lips brushing against his cock as she spoke.

"Well, since you asked so nicely," he quipped and brought the vibe to life at its highest setting. Before she could even form a thought, she was already cumming again. As her orgasm receded, she expected him to turn the vibe off, but he did not. He only fucked her throat savagely, She could feel some drool begin to dribble out of her mouth and down his shaft, but she was so drunk on lust that she didn't care. She was beyond all words and all thought. He was in control, and she was his puppet. As he thrust into her throat hard and fast, she climaxed again and again, losing track of how many times she came. It seemed to go on forever.

"Daddy's dirty little cocksucker," he

growled, his growing stiffer. "You're going to make me cum, princess." He grabbed her by her hair, pulling her off his shaft and looming over her. He worked his cock furiously over her open mouth and let loose all over her face. It was sensual and erotic, the way his hot seed rained down over her, and she caught as much as she could in her mouth, savoring the taste of him. He sighed with satisfaction as his orgasm receded. Still gripping her tightly by the hair, he brought her face to his, kissing her deeply as his ragged breath returned to a normal pace.

"Oh kitten, you look so pretty covered in my cum."

"Thank you, Daddy," she said, glowing at the compliment. Indeed, she did feel pretty, even tied up and coated with sticky cum. If that was how he liked her, then she was proud to oblige him. He scooped some of it off of her face, feeding it to her with his fingers, smirking at the way she eagerly gobbled it up. He left most of it on her face, her badge of honor, and put the ball gag back into her mouth and zipped himself up again.

"Stay just like that, princess," he said, as if she had any choice in the matter, and turned his attention back to his work.

Chapter 13

He kept her like that for a long time until her muscles ached, and she began to grow restless. Occasionally, he watched her squirm against her restraints, seemingly lost in thought but then he would return his attention to his work and ignore her once more. Finally, he turned his computer off and crossed the short distance from the desk to the settee. He took a moment to admire her one last time, bound and helpless, before gently removing the ball gag. She stretched her aching jaw, happy to be free.

"You did a very good job today, kitten," he said gently as he began to untie her. "Daddy is very proud of you." His praise made the sore muscles in her thighs more than worth it. Once she was freed from the rope, she stretched her limbs as well. With a quick kiss on her forehead, he bundled her up in his arms and carried her off to the bathroom. He drew a bubble bath for her, holding her hand as she got in, her legs still shaky. The warm water felt amazing on her stiff muscles, and she leaned back, surrendering to the relaxing sensations. His large hands began to massage her scalp, sending her even further into relaxed bliss. He moved his hands down to her shoulders, kneading the tense muscles until they released under his strong grip. Once she was in a total zenlike state, he cleaned her from head to toe with a loofah, carefully washing away all of the cum and sweat from her skin. He washed her hair next, rinsing out the suds with some water from a plastic cup. She leaned back, letting the warm water cascade over her hair. Once she was all clean, he spent some time rubbing her feet, letting her relax in the warm water while he eased any remaining tension away. Eventually, he let out the water and bundled her body and hair into towels before carrying her to her grownup bed.

As he lowered her onto the bed, he lowered

himself on top of her and kissed her lips, her petite frame melting against him, her soft tongue tenderly seeking out his. His hands cupped her cheeks, savoring her for a moment, before lowering them down to wrap around her throat. Instantly, her entire body was flooded with hot desire. Malcolm could feel the needful heat radiating off her skin as he tightened his grip. Her hands sought out his cock, caressing the length of his hardness through his pants as he choked her. He parted her legs by forcing his knees between them. In her relaxed state, Amber couldn't stop herself from rubbing her aching pussy against his thigh like an animal in heat. He chuckled and watched her writhe against him with satisfaction.

"Still greedy, my pet?" he growled into her ear. She nodded. He released her throat and brought his cock to her lips. "I want your mouth again. Suck my cock, my dirty girl." She obeyed, moaning at the taste of him. He put his hands on the back of her head, guiding the pace and the depth as she relaxed and let him fuck her throat.

She wanted to touch herself, but he knew she would wait until he gave her permission.

"Good slut," he said, letting her know just how proud he was of her. Her eyes rolled back in her head, his words making her pussy feel like it was on fire. He withdrew his cock from her mouth and placed it between her ample tits. Slick with her saliva, he began to slide it between them.

"You may touch yourself," he said, knowing that being used like this would drive her wild. He squeezed her tits tight around his member and let himself enjoy her body. "Good girl. Such a good girl." The sight of his hard cock disappearing into her cleavage over and over was just too sexy, and he felt himself getting close to the edge. Too close. He pulled his cock back and wrapped his hands around her throat once again.

"Fuck yourself," he commanded, and she plunged her fingers into her cunt, pumping them in and out furiously. She was quickly approaching the edge, as well.

"You want to cum, kitten?" he asked

teasingly. She nodded and fucked herself faster.

"Stop!" At his command, her hands left her cunt, and her entire being shuddered at the sudden interruption.

"That was a question, not an order. Do you want to cum?"

"Yes, Daddy,' she whimpered.

"Good girl. You may cum on my cock," he said. She turned around and got on all fours. He knelt and entered swiftly, impatient to be inside of her again. She had the tightest pussy he had ever fucked, not to mention the fact that her enthusiasm was very addictive. It was tempting to unload inside of her then and there, but he wanted to make her cum one last time before her nap. Pounding into her, he could feel pussy tighten as her orgasm began to surface, but he wanted to make it last just a little while longer, torment her with pleasure just a little bit longer. Finally, he couldn't hold back any longer.

"Cum now!" he commanded, and he could

feel her tighten and shudder against him in relief. He let go too, throwing his head back as they pulsed and quivered together. She was already yawning as he eased her onto the covers, wrapping them around her burrito style. He kissed her on the cheek and watched her for a moment, her face already slack with exhaustion. He had completely worn her out.

"Enjoy your nap, little one," he whispered. "You earned it."

***

She awoke sometime later to a dark and silent room. She listened for him but didn't hear anything outside of the room either. She didn't get up right away, spending some time to reflect on what happened earlier. It was almost like having someone else's memories as she remembered how wanton she had been, so completely uninhibited. She had never done anything that wild before. The memory made her grow hungry once again, despite how many times she had orgasmed that day. Daddy had called her so many dirty things as he used her, and she had loved every moment of it. The way that he degraded her and used her as a toy was so erotic. The memory made her moan, and her fingers dipped down to her pussy before she could catch herself. She was still slick with his cum, which only made her hornier. She told herself it was only for a second, but she couldn't bring herself to stop touching it. Warm waves of pleasure washed over her as she flicked the tender nub with her fingertip. Riding closer and closer to the edge, she closed her eyes and let herself enjoy the sensations.

I'll stop before I cum like a good girl. She promised herself silently. *Just another couple of seconds.*

"Stop!" Malcolm's voice was loud and angry. She jerked her hand away and opened her eyes to see him standing at the foot of her bed, frowning with his hands on his hips. He was shirtless and only wearing a pair of black pressed slacks, water still dripping from his hair as though he had just stepped out of the shower.

"Bad girl!"

"Daddy! I- I-" she stuttered, knowing that she had been caught red-handed and wouldn't be able to talk her way out of it.

"Did I give you permission to touch yourself?" She did her best to ignore how sexy he looked with wet hair and no shirt and answered him in a quiet, shy voice.

"No, Daddy." She avoided his gaze, her face growing hot with shame.

"No, I certainly did not. Then why do you have your fingers in Daddy's toy? I'm sorry to have to do this, but you've been a very naughty little girl, and Daddy is going to have to punish you." He scooped her up in his arms, still naked, and carried her to her little girl room. There, he put her down firmly on one of the chairs surrounding the small table, and Amber chewed on her lip and wondered what kind of punishment he had in mind. He grabbed a notepad and a brown crayon from the shelf, both of which he put down on the table in front of her. Even his color choice was a punishment, she noticed.

"Write this down: 'I will not touch myself without Daddy's permission.'" Picking up the crayon with a shaky hand, she wrote the words down slowly and carefully. He watched over her shoulder and gave a single short nod when she had finished.

"Good. Now, I want you to write that forty times. Don't leave this chair until it's done. Bring it to me when you finish." He left her to begin her task and closed the door behind him. Obediently, Amber began copying the words. The crayon made the letters look sloppy and childish, which seemed fitting to her. She made sure to go slowly and take her time, not wanting to make any mistakes. Despite her best efforts, she did make a mistake on the sixteenth line, writing an "a" instead of an "o." She tore the page out and crumpled it up, starting again on a fresh sheet of paper. By the time she reached line thirty, her hand began to cramp.

Determined to push through the discomfort, she finished the second draft with no mistakes. Breathing a sigh of relief, she stood and got dressed, picking out an especially cute outfit in the hopes that it would earn her a little extra credit. She picked up the completed assignment, carrying it down the hall to present to Malcolm. He was sitting on the couch in the living room reading a newspaper, which he put down when Amber presented him with her work. He studied it carefully, reading it line by line. As he read, she noticed that he was now wearing a crisp button-down and that his hair had been neatly combed into place. Once he finished, he nodded and put it down.

"The second part of your punishment is to receive forty lashes with a belt on your bottom." Amber's jaw went slack with surprise.

"F-forty?!" she stuttered. Her tummy suddenly felt all fluttery, and her palms prickled with sweat.

"That's right. Bad girls who touch

themselves have to learn their lesson." He stood and removed his belt slowly, the leather making a wsssk sound as it passed through the loops on his trousers. As nervous as she was about her forty licks, the sight did excite her just a little. He sat back down again and motioned to his lap.

"Get over Daddy's knee, little girl." She swallowed nervously but did as she was told. As she settled onto his lap, he lifted up her skirt, exposing her bare bottom. He ran his hands over her flesh, raising goosebumps as he did so.

"Every time Daddy gives you a lick, I want you to count. Do you understand?"

"Yes, Daddy," she said. Without any further warning, he brought the belt down hard, exploding sharp pain onto her tender skin. Hot tears sprang to her eyes, and she gasped out loud.

"One," she managed to choke out, despite the sob trying to escape. The second blow came quickly, causing her to jerk from the burning pain.

"Two," she sobbed, squirming in his lap as he delivered blow after blow. She counted each one out loud, kicking and crying the entire time. The more she cried and squirmed and kicked, the harder she could feel Daddy's cock grow against her stomach. By the time he was through, her ass was bright red and covered in welts. He ran his hands lightly over her bruised skin, breathing heavily as he examined his handiwork. His fingers delved into her folds, groaning at the wetness he found there.

"Oh kitten, did your spanking make you horny?"

"Yes, Daddy," she confessed, hoping that wouldn't make him want to come up with a different way to punish her instead.

"Good," he said curtly. "Now, bend over." She bent over the couch, putting her hands down on the cushions but that wasn't what he had in mind. He pushed her face down into the couch cushions and got behind her. With her butt stuck up in the air, she felt incredibly exposed and vulnerable. She shivered with anticipation, wondering what he would do next. He hiked up her skirt and spread her stinging cheeks. She felt his hot, wet tongue against her pussy lips. He moaned as he explored her wet folds, enjoying the taste of her for a moment before working his way up. The tip of his tongue flicked against her bum, making her gasp. He spread her cheeks apart, burying his face deeper. His fingers digging into her bruised flesh stung but the pain only made the pleasure all the sweeter. A little moan escaped her lips as she leaned back onto that hot, wet tongue as it awoke a desire in her that she had never felt before. Once her rear entrance was nice and wet, he began to explore her with his fingers, stretching out her little hole bit by bit. She groaned and pushed back onto his exploring digits, craving more.

"You like that, naughty girl?" he asked.

"Yes, Daddy."

"Are you ready to take Daddy's cock in your ass?" He pulled his fingers out and started rubbing the head of his cock against her opening. She hesitated, wanting to feel that monster cock inside of her but also feeling a bit trepidatious.

"It's so big, Daddy. Will it fit?"

"Don't worry. I'll make it fit." The head of his cock slowly began to enter her and Amber tried her best to relax into it. Pain and pleasure swirled together in an intoxicating cocktail as she took deep breaths. He paused, barely inside of her and let her body adjust to this new intrusion.

"That's it, baby girl. Just relax and let Daddy in." He began to push a little further in, making her gasp as he stretched her tight asshole open. His fingers gripped her buttocks, spreading her flesh apart as he slowly impaled her. As he went deeper, she could feel herself relaxing more, accepting his presence in her virgin ass, and the pleasure started to become the dominant sensation over the pain.

"Oh princess, your ass is so tight around Daddy's cock!" he cried out, thrusting into her. He was finally entirely enveloped by her, and he started to very slowly pump in and out of her with small movements. Amber groaned loudly, feeling like he was going to split her in two. She had never felt so stretched, so filled. His strokes began to get a little longer, and Amber felt the need for release. Her moans must have betrayed her because he gave her a warning smack on the ass.

"No cumming, little one. You're still in trouble." Amber whimpered in disappointment. His cock felt so good, and she was so turned on, but she knew that she must be a good girl if she was going to get back into his good graces. "Now, take your ass fucking like a good little slut." He was fucking her hard and fast now, every stroke sending waves of pleasure all over her body. The way he grunted and cussed told Amber that he wouldn't last much longer. Sure enough, he gripped her by the hair and pulled her back onto his cock as he slammed into her. The combination of pain and ecstasy almost sent her over the edge, but she held back.

"Fuck, Daddy's going to cum in your tight little ass, princess!" She gasped as his cock swelled and twitched, pumping hot jizz deep inside of her. He shuddered and leaned all of his weight onto her, pinning her against the couch as the final waves of his orgasm washed over him. He kissed the back of her sweaty neck and pulled himself out of her with a heavy sigh. He pulled her butt cheeks apart once again and watched with satisfaction as his seed trickled out of her and down her thigh.

"You liked being Daddy's little anal whore, didn't you princess? I bet you're just dying to cum," he said teasingly. Amber nodded, her pussy was still aching with need, and she would give just about anything to be allowed to cum all over Daddy's big cock.

"You should have thought about that before you misbehaved. Now, go clean yourself up. It's time for dinner."

Chapter 14

When she came downstairs, he already had dinner on the table.

"You took your punishment like a good girl. Did you learn your lesson?" She nodded, looking up at him with wide, wet eyes.

"Yes, Daddy," she said meekly.

"Good girl, Daddy is very proud of you." He kissed her on her forehead and pulled out her chair for her to sit. She devoured her dinner, finding that she was ravenously hungry. He watched her with amusement, eating his own dinner slowly. When she sat back with a satisfied sigh, full at last, he was still working his way through his.

"While you were sleeping, I found an open casting call for a local theater group. It's tomorrow at two. You're going," he said with finality. "I printed out the details so you can look over them." She smiled, absolutely amused that he was pretending to be stern when he was doing something incredibly kind, scouring the internet for acting opportunities for her to follow up on.

"Thank you, Daddy," she said, kissing him on the cheek. He continued eating his dinner, steadfastly ignoring the blush that come over his face.

***

She spent the rest of the evening studying lines. She had standard monologue that she usually auditioned with, but she didn't feel like it was appropriate for the dramatic role she was hoping to land. Finally, Malcolm had to drag her away practically.

"Give your brain a rest, little one," he advised. "Come on, let's have a few beers on the couch and then head to bed early. What do you say?" She smiled shyly, knowing that he was right.

She wasn't doing herself any favors by wearing herself out.

"Sounds good, Daddy." Half a beer later, Amber rested her head drowsily on his shoulder as he rubbed her back absentmindedly.

"You have nothing to worry about, little one. You are very talented, and I know that they'll see that and offer you the role right away." The beer was making her head swim, and his light, soothing touch was very relaxing. His warmth emanating through his crisp pressed clothes was oddly comforting, as were his soothing words, and she closed her eyes while he gently explored her body. His fingertips traveled down her legs, tickled her knees, then traced their way back up her tummy and lightly brushing her nipples through her shirt. She nuzzled her face further into his neck to hide her blushing cheeks and giggled quietly, suddenly feeling very shy. Putting his beer down on the coffee table, he cupped her face with his hand and lifted her face so that she had to look at him.

"Don't hide," he whispered. "You're very sexy, kitten." He cupped her breast lightly and chuckled as her cheeks once again turned pink. She held his gaze, though, just as he instructed, her big eyes locked onto his as his hands began to travel downward once more. He dipped his hand between her legs and cupped it against her mound. It radiated with heat as the desire that always seemed to be lying dormant just beneath the surface was beginning to reignite. She gave a tiny little moan and ground her crotch into his palm.

"Poor, needy little baby! You're practically dripping into my hand. Does Daddy's little slut need to cum?" She gasped as he dipped a finger into her slit, overwhelmed by her need for him.

"Yes, Daddy! I need to cum so bad! Please, let me. Please!" The ache that had been building all evening was so great that she didn't care that she was begging. She would beg all night if it brought her the release she needed. He withdrew his finger, slick with her lust, and put it in her mouth.

"Taste how desperate you are, little one.

Suck your juices off Daddy's fingers." Obediently, she suckled, tasting her own sweet nectar, moaning at the taste. He pushed his fingers deeper into her mouth and down her throat, choking her. She gagged, but he only pushed deeper, watching her throat bulge around his intruding digits. As he pulled his hand out, drool dribbled down her lips and chin.

"Does Daddy's greedy little baby want to touch herself?" he asked, teasingly. She felt like she could cum at the slightest stimulation, and the need for release was growing too intense for her to deny any longer.

"Yes, Daddy. Please, may I touch myself? I need it so bad." She pleaded with both her words and her eyes, begging him to end her torture.

"Spread your legs," he commanded sharply. She complied instantly, spreading her legs widely. With her pussy exposed, she waited for his next command.

"You may touch yourself, but you had better not cum until I tell you to." Eagerly, she pressed on her clit, delighting in the delicious waves that washed over her as her finger slipped around her sensitive nub. Her buzz only enhanced the sensations, making her even more attuned to the ecstasy she was providing for herself.

"That's it, kitten," he said, his voice thick with lust. "Now, put one of your fingers inside your tight pussy." With a grunt, she thrust her finger in her dripping folds, pumping it in and out.

"Slow down, greedy. I told you not to cum yet, remember?" Amber whimpered and pouted, but slowed down any way. "That's it, pumpkin." She bit her lip, concentrating on how nice it felt to have her aching pussy get some attention at last. She was already close to the edge, yet her slender finger didn't feel like quite enough anymore after experiencing his thick cock. She thought about how he stretched and filled her and moaned out loud.

"Mmm, good girl. Now touch your clit again." Her finger traveled upwards once more, and she shivered as she pressed against her most sensitive spot. "I know you're dripping wet. I can smell your sweet honey from here. You must really need to cum. Does Daddy's dirty little slut need to cum?" His words made her thrust her hips upwards, excitement coursing through her at the prospect of being allowed a release at last.

"Yes, Daddy. Please let me cum. I need it so bad." Her pace quickened, twirling around her swollen nub and pushing herself dangerously close to the edge.

"Are you close, baby girl?" He leaned closer to her, and she could feel his intense gaze tracking her movements as she obeyed his every command. His breath was heavy against her neck, sending warm tingles all over her body.

"Yes, Daddy. I'm very close. So, so close. Please!" Her voice was starting to take on a whiny quality, but she didn't care. He didn't answer her, only watched her writhe on couch cushions. She could feel her orgasm building. Either she would have to stop touching herself soon, or there would be no stopping it, no matter how hard she tried.

Her legs quivered from the effort of holding herself back, and her soft moans were getting louder and louder.

"Stop!" he growled. Reluctantly, she pulled her hand away. Without thinking, she closed her legs, wanting to feel the pressure of her thighs against her throbbing clit. "Open those legs, baby girl. I'm not done with you yet." Slowly, she extended her legs once again. She clenched her fists by her side, resisting the urge to plunge her fingers back inside of her before he told her to. He watched her for a moment, letting her suffer before sliding his finger into her needy cunt, eliciting a high pitched moan from Amber.

"Is that what Daddy's greedy little slut wanted?" he teased. She couldn't answer in words, so she nodded her head and gripped her thighs. His fingers felt even better than hers. He slipped a second finger inside of her, pumping in and out firmly. "Use your words, pumpkin." Amber bit her lip, her cheeks burning. Her hands released her thighs and covered her face instead.

"Nngh, yes! Daddy's greedy little slut wants to cum. Please, please, please, can I please?" Her words tumbled out rapidly as she grew more and more frantic.

"You're such a good girl. You may cum if you want to, little one." With a cry of relief, Amber threw her head back and surrendered herself to the intense pleasure. Her orgasm broke over her in waves, and she squealed into her hands as her thighs quivered, and her back arched. Hours of sexual tension finally released, Amber sagged back against the couch, but he didn't remove his hand. The climax had made her extra sensitive she instinctively tried to close her legs to block his access but he only slapping her thighs, forcing them open again.

"If you try to close those legs again, I will tie them open again. I already told you, I'm not done with you yet." She whimpered as he continued to fuck her with his fingers, but he was unmoved.

"I thought this is what you wanted, kitten. You were begging to cum just a minute ago. I don't think you've had enough yet." He curled his fingers upwards, seeking the very center of her pleasure. She gasped and bit down on her thumb as his fingers thrust into her with an insistent, unyielding rhythm.

"That's it, sweetie. Be a good little slut and cum for Daddy again." He knew just how and where to touch her to get exactly what he wanted, and within moments, another orgasm was ripping through her, her legs and arms flailing against the overwhelming ecstasy.

"Good girl," he purred, and before she knew it, he was pushing her down onto the couch, his big thick cock pushing into her. For once, he was the impatient one, and he filled her up in one motion. As his girth spread and filled her, she could feel another climax already building.

"You're such a greedy little slut, aren't you? No matter how many times I make you cum, you're still hungry for more." He slammed into her, leaving no part of her untouched as he filled her over and over. Unable to hold back, she came undone on his cock, babbling and thrashing against him as he kept the same steady pace. Each time she came was more intense than the last, each one leaving her even more sensitive to the steady pounding of his cock.

"God, you're so tight, princess. Do you like being a slut for Daddy?"

"Yes, Daddy," she said with a shaky voice. "I love being your slut. Fuck your little slut, Daddy." With a growl, he abandoned his steady rhythm and began fucking her hard and fast. She could feel his cock start to swell and knew that he was close to the edge. As his cock split her open, she could feel one last orgasm mounting.

"Cum inside me, Daddy," she pleaded and gripped his buttocks to pull him deeper inside. "I love it when you give me your cum." He cried out, and as he pumped his hot juices inside of her, she had the most intense pleasure she had ever experienced. Her entire body felt electric, and she was still twitching with ecstasy long after he had stilled inside of her. With a contented sigh, he withdrew, sitting up on the couch. She lay her head down in his lap and he pet her hair while her breath slowly returned to normal.

"Do you see now why Daddy makes you wait sometimes? Wasn't it worth it?" His fingers combed through her hair and massaged her scalp tenderly.

"Yes, Daddy," she said dreamily. "You're always right."

Chapter 15

The next afternoon, Amber practically ran down the sidewalk, bursting with the good news. The elevator seemed even slower than normal, and she tapped her foot impatiently. At last, she burst into the living room where Malcolm was waiting, a nervous expression carved onto his face.

"Well?!" he asked before she could even get her jacket off. "What did they say?" She grinned at him, almost too giddy to get the words out.

"I got it!" she exclaimed. "I got the lead part." His face lit up, and he wrapped her up in a tight bear hug, sweeping her off her feet and swinging her around until she squealed.

"I knew you would," he said smugly as he put her down again. "See, I told you that Daddy is always right. When do you start?"

"Next week," she said. She chewed her lip,

feeling a bit nervous to tell him this next part. "And it's eight shows a week, so I'm afraid it might interfere with my duties as your assistant. I hope that's ok." Suddenly his face got serious. He took her hand and led her over to the couch, motioning for her to sit.

"That's actually something I've been meaning to talk to you about. I'm really glad that you have this acting job to fall back on because I'm afraid that I'm going to have to fire you." Her heart sank as she stared at him in shock. Fired?! Her mind raced, trying to find where she had gone wrong, why he didn't want her anymore. Before she could ask any questions, he continued speaking.

"You see, I want to ask you to be my girlfriend, but you really shouldn't date your employees," She laughed as a wave of relief washed over her, and she slapped his arm, cutting him off.

"That was dirty, Daddy!" she yelled at him between giggles. "You nearly gave me a heart attack, you big meanie." He chuckled, defending himself from her playful swats.

"I surrender, I surrender," he said, pulling her close. "So it that a yes? You'll be my baby girl really and truly?"

"Yes, Daddy," she said, smiling up at him. "I'll be your baby girl really and truly." He kissed her gently, cupping her face lovingly. Even that gentle, loving touch was enough to ignite her desire. She moaned and ran her fingers through his hair, opening her mouth for his tongue.

"What's the matter, princess? Are you starting to feel tingly in your private parts again?" he whispered. They hadn't fucked before her audition, Malcolm said that she should reserve her energy. Now that she was past that hurdle, she was eager to make up for the lost time, even if it was only a few hours. She nodded and bit her lip. "Well, since you've been such a good girl today, I'll let you suck me off." She kneeled in front of him, unzipping his pants to release his monster cock. She took a moment to lovingly nuzzle the cock that she had missed so much all day. He stroked her hair as she wrapped her lips around the tip of his member and swirled her tongue around him, delighting in how his eyes rolled back and a gruff moan escaped his lips. Unable to hold herself back, she swallowed his cock deeply, his member pulsing inside of her tight, warm throat. Pushing past her gag reflex, she worked him in and out of her mouth, swallowing him deeply with every stroke. He gripped her hair, encouraging her to take him faster and deeper, fucking her face with abandon.

"That's a good girl. Make Daddy cum with your mouth, sweetheart." She moaned around his hardness, caressing his balls lightly as she quickened her pace and pushed herself to take him even deeper. As her lips began to graze the very root of his cock, she could feel his testicles tighten, and he pumped his hot jizz deep into her throat, his hands gripping her hair so tightly that it hurt. It was too much for her to swallow, and as he pulled his cock from her mouth, his creamy white cum dribbled out of her mouth and onto her shirt. He chuckled indulgently.

"What a silly, drooly baby you are." He caught some of the jizz that dangled from her chin and fed it back to her, her eager tongue lapping her reward from his salty palms. "I'm tempted to make you wear that cum soaked shirt out tonight so that everyone sees that you're Daddy's spoiled little slave. Say it."

"I'm Daddy's spoiled little slave." She grinned up at him, and he rewarded her with a deep kiss, his tongue lazily her exploring her mouth. "Now get up and show Daddy how wet you are." She stood and proudly lifted her skirt, stepping her feet wide so that he could pull her labia apart and inspect her closely. She was soaking wet from sucking his cock, and the inspection made her pussy tingle all the more.

"Mmm, good girl, I can see you're on your way to being a desperate, drippy mess. Just how I like you. That will have to wait until later. We've got two things to celebrate tonight. Go put on something sexy, baby girl. We're going out tonight."

***

They stumbled back to his apartment sometime later. He had spent the entire night bragging to every stranger that they saw that his girlfriend was going to be a famous actress, something that never failed to make her blush and giggle. They had both drank more than they probably should have, giddy both at her success and their newfound love. Both were reasonably buzzed by the time they got back, so they fumbled with each other's clothes at the same time, giggling and groping each other as they went. Somehow, they managed to get upstairs and into Malcolm's bed. Amber was already most of the way out of her dress, and he jumped at the chance to suck on one of her perky breasts. She moaned at the ripples of pleasure that started at his mouth and ended at her aching pussy. He pulled her dress the rest of the way down as he worked her nipple between his teeth. The pain made her back arch and her folds flooded with desire.

"My dirty girl," he whispered approvingly. He grazed his index finger over her slippery-wet clit. She writhed beneath him and moaned pleadingly. He rolled off of her momentarily, which made her pout. She was even needier and hornier when drunk, it turned out. He chuckled at her neediness and took his pants off, kicking them to the other side of the room. A wicked smile took the place of her pout as she leaned over him, eyeing his cock hungrily. She licked the tip of his hardness and wrapped her lips around him, moaning as she took him further down. She loved how wild with need it made her feel when she asphyxiated herself on his hardness. He pushed himself further down her throat, knowing by now exactly where her limit was and rode the edge as far as he could before pulling her back up by her hair. She managed to take a deep breath before he plunged his cock back into her mouth. He grabbed a fistful of hair and twisted as he thrust into her throat over and over, fucking her face. The pain and domination canceled all thoughts in her head and transformed her into a blank slate of hazy pleasure, eager to serve him for as long as he would let her.

"Touch your pussy," he commanded. She relished the sensation of her velvety smoothness beneath her fingers as she obeyed him. Her fingers traveled easily over her wet pussy, exploring her clit and hungry hole. He jammed his cock hard down her throat and held it there while she gagged and choked. She plunged two fingers into her cunt and fucked herself wildly. Even two fingers weren't enough to satisfy her anymore, however. What she needed was Malcolm. He couldn't hold himself back anymore and let himself unload down her throat. She eagerly swallowed his seed and giggled as she wiped away some that had dripped out onto her lips.

"Your turn," he growled, pushing her back

onto the bed and diving between her legs.

"Thank you, Daddy," she moaned and spread her legs eagerly for him.

"I love the way you eat my pussy." He leaned down and gently pressed his lips against her slick folds. For a moment, he merely breathed her in, savoring the fresh scent and heat of her arousal. Amber had never felt so sexy as she did when he used her like that. He made her feel so exposed and vulnerable yet quivering with electric anticipation. His tongue dove into her folds, intimately familiar by now with every inch of her, knowing all of her most sensitive spots. His tongue was so warm, so wet, and he seemed to delight in teasing her until her entire body felt like it was burning with lust. His strong hands gripped her thighs and held her legs open. She writhed and moaned beneath him, gasping "Daddy!" over and over as her arousal built. He pulled her swollen clit into his mouth, flicking it with his tongue. She buried her sweaty, trembling fingers in his hair instead, drawing him closer.

"Fuck, Daddy! That feels so good!" Her thighs tried to close around him, but he merely dug his fingers deeper into her flesh and kept them pinned in place. Her feeble efforts were no match for his strength, and that realization, along with the dull pain from his grip, pushed her closer to her climax. She loved how helpless he made her feel.

"Please, Daddy. May I pretty please cum? You feel so good, Daddy!" she pleaded, gripping his shoulders as she held herself back and waited for his permission. He didn't answer her at first. Instead, he plunged two fingers into her slit and pumped them in and out of her while he continued to tongue her clit. It took every ounce of her willpower not to explode then and there. Every one of her muscles clenched as she rode the edge of climax, determined to wait like a good girl until he gave her permission. Her obedience was soon rewarded.

"You may cum now," he whispered against her before pressing his tongue into her clit once more. She finally succumbed to the waves of pleasure that had been building up, her body convulsing as she gripped him by the hair and rode his tongue to orgasm. He growled with satisfaction, quickening his pace, wanting to completely overwhelm her with pleasure. Her muscles at last unclenched and she lay panting and shivering.

"You taste so good, pumpkin," he murmured and nuzzled her inner thighs as she recovered from her intense experience. His kisses began to travel upwards, across her firm tummy, up her ribcage, around her breasts, and up her neck. Their lips met, his tongue intertwined with hers. Nestled between her legs, she could feel that he was already hard again. With a grunt, he grabbed her hand and guided it to his hardness, shivering slightly as she gripped him.

"You see what you do to Daddy, little girl?" he rasped, his voice thick with lust. "That's because you're so, so sexy." She stroked him, delighting in the way it made his brow wrinkle and his breath to get ragged. He buried his face in her neck, kissing and licking her neck while she played with his member, her hands exploring his hardness, his balls, his everything, so happy to have him for her very own. As his excitement grew, so did hers, and she was once again consumed by an untamed desire. She longed to have his cock inside of her and rubbed his swollen head against her silky, wet folds. He grunted and grabbed a fistful of her hair, making her groan in response. She guided him to her slick opening, and he pressed in slowly. Her fingers dug into his buttocks as he inched his length inside of her. Once he was completely sheathed inside of her, she felt all of her inhibitions melting away.

"Oh, Daddy. Fuck me! Fuck me hard, please!" she cried out and pulled his hips closer. He began to move inside of her, the walls of her pussy hugging him so tight it was hard not release himself deep in her wetness. He twisted his fist in her hair and pumped into her. She began squealing and babbling, her mind and body totally awash with the intense pleasure of his thick cock spreading her, filling her up so deep, his hardness driving into her needy core. He pressed his forehead into hers and pinned her wrists against the bed, enjoying the feeling of possessing her completely.

"You're mine, baby girl. All. Mine." He punctuated his words with hard thrusts into her hot tightness. Her eyes rolled back, and she continued to stutter incoherently. Occasionally, he could make out the words "fuck" and "yes" and "Daddy" but she mostly seemed beyond words, beyond thought, consumed instead with pure animalistic hunger.

"You're doing such a good job, baby," he said huskily. "You're being such a good slut for Daddy, letting him use your tight little pussy. I'm so proud of you, little one." Amber came again, even harder than before, his dirty words filling her with a delicious heat that permeated throughout her entire being and left her shivering and quaking. He rutted his hips against hers, realizing that he wouldn't be able to hold back much longer as her orgasm made her grip him even tighter.

"Daddy's going to cum inside you, Princess. I'm going to fill you up, baby. Here it comes." His cock twitched, and he couldn't hold back a shuddering grunt as he pumped his hot, sticky seed inside of her. Collapsing into a sweaty, trembling mess, he lay panting against her neck as she caressed his hair and kissed his salty forehead. After a moment, he withdrew from her and scooped her up into his arms, kissing her deeply.

"You're such a good girl," he whispered silkily into her hair and wrapped her tightly in his arms. "I'm so lucky to have you." She relaxed into the safety of his arms, wrapped up in a cocoon of hazy contentment. He held her until her eyes began to get heavy once again. When it was apparent that she was falling asleep, he pulled the covers over them and kissed her on the forehead.

"I love you, Amber," he whispered in her ear, his voice trembling as he said it.

"I love you too, Daddy," she murmured sleepily, wrapping her arms tightly around his neck.

Chapter 16

Amber officially moved in with Malcolm right away and signed her lease over to Leslie's co-worker. She let the girl take the pick of her furniture and sold the rest, not seeing much point in putting it in storage. Malcolm told her not to worry about pitching in for rent, which was a relief. She didn't know exactly how much he paid, but from the look of his apartment, there was no way she could ever afford it. Thanks to his generosity, she was able to pay Leslie back the money she owed her which was a huge relief to Amber. Leslie had been so kind to her when they were roommates, and she deserved to have that kindness repaid. The play ran much longer than expected, selling out every night for weeks on end. Many of the reviews singled her out by name, giving her credit for the success of the show. After struggling for so long for a breakthrough, it was amazingly gratifying to see her name in print at last. Every night, Malcolm was right in the front row, silently cheering her on. Even when the show was extended and he had seen the show enough times to know it by heart, he was still right there, looking just as proud of her as he had the first night. The final evening of the show, Malcolm gave her a giant bouquet of flowers as the crowd gave her a standing ovation. It was so gratifying to have the man she loved supporting her as she achieved her dreams. It was one of the many reasons why she loved him so much. It was late when she finally said all of her goodbyes and graciously accepted all of her congratulations. They decided to walk home that evening, wanting to enjoy the lovely, warm evening and get some fresh air. He wrapped his arm around her waist as they walked and talked, occasionally stopping to look at the window displays in the shops. It was the first time she had gotten just to enjoy the city since she moved there and she was glad that she was seeing it with him.

"I'm so proud of you, baby girl," he said and squeezed her tightly. "You looked so beautiful up there on that stage. You're definitely going to be a star after this, I just know it." She blushed but hoped that he was right. *Daddy's always right;* she reminded herself and smiled.

"Thank you, Daddy," she said and sniffed her bouquet, remembering how fun the entire experience was and how she couldn't wait to do it again. She didn't need to be a star, not really, but she did hope that she gained a good enough reputation to maintain steady work. Eventually, they passed an alley, and Malcolm slowed his pace. He looked cautiously down the alley, making sure that it was completely empty before looking at her with a naughty glint in his eye. She recognized the look and immediately knew what was on his mind. He loved fucking her in public, and she loved to let him. He took her by the hand and pulled her toward the alley. She looked over her shoulder to make sure that no one saw and followed him, already feeling a tingle between her legs. Once they were in the shadows, he stood behind her and began to run his hands over her curves. She leaned into him, eager for him already.

"You really did look beautiful up there, kitten," he whispered in her ear. She moaned and ground her ass against his crotch, delighting in the way it made him sigh. "You're the sexiest woman in the world. You know that?" She nodded, knowing that in his mind, it was true. He was always telling her how beautiful and sexy he found her, always telling her that she was the woman of his dreams and she never got tired of hearing.

"Good girl," he growled. "Now pull up your skirt." Her clit was throbbing as she did what he commanded, her shaking hands pulled her skirt up over the swell of her ass, exposing herself to the dim light of the alleyway. She faced the wall and waited, her skin tingling with anticipation. He knew how much waiting made her crazy, which was why he delayed her pleasure so frequently.

"Now pull down your panties," he

commanded next. Eagerly, she pulled down her thong, her pussy already aching for him. As he groped her bare ass, she heard the sound of metal on metal as he unzipped his pants, and she moaned, knowing what was coming next.

"Bend over," he said. She put her hand on the wall to steady herself and bent at the hips, giving him a full view of her pussy and ass. She loved showing off for him, loved the hungry look he always got for her. He made a satisfied noise and began running his cock along her crack. She moaned and thrust her hips back, craving to have his thick cock inside of her.

"You want to be fucked in a back alley like some dirty little slut, little one?" He pressed his hard cock against her clit as he teased her, making her legs tremble slightly. He laughed as he tapped it against her slick folds, making her jump and twitch with every tap. She nearly yelped at the sensation but bit her lip and stayed quiet lest she spoiled their game by getting caught.

"Oh kitten, you're already so wet and needy

for Daddy's cock. You just can't get enough of it, can you?" She shook her head and groaned, squirming back against him. It was true. They fucked constantly yet she still craved him nearly all of the time.

"No, Daddy, I can never get enough of your cock. I need you to fuck me, please."

"Good girl," he sighed, inching himself into her slowly. Her eyes rolled back in her head as he slowly filled her, burying himself in her completely. He held her there for a moment, grabbing her by the hips as he savored the feeling of being so deep inside of her. As he pulled out, he deliberately keeping his pace as slow as possible to drive her crazy. Amber whimpered quietly as he slowly stretched her open, pleasuring her but also leaving her aching for more. She thrust her hips back in an attempt to increase the tempo, but he only slapped her ass to keep her in line.

"Slow down, little one," he warned. "Don't want you getting too excited. I know how loud you can get, and we don't want the whole world to know that you're a dirty little slut who likes to get fucked in back alleys, now do we?" Her pussy tightened around him, his words only making her crave him all the more. She couldn't deny that she could get quite loud indeed, especially when he said dirty things like that to her. She whined and gripped the wall as he fucked her in his own sweet time, seemingly not the least bit concerned that they could be discovered at any moment even with her being quiet.

"I'll be quiet, Daddy," she promised. "Please fuck me harder." He made a strangled noise and slammed his cock into her, suddenly pounding fast and hard, no more teasing. She held on tight, biting her lip to keep from screaming. Every thrust sent a lightning bolt of pleasure through her, and all she was aware of was how much she loved the dirty things he did to her and how good it felt to be his and his alone.

"Good girl," he whispered. "That's a good little slut." Suddenly, he was pulsing inside of her, grunting as he pumped her full of his seed. It felt so amazing, the way he filled her up, her reward for a job well done. She felt like she would never get enough of his hot cum, no matter how many times they fucked. As he pulled out of her, he was careful to catch all the semen that dripped out onto her panties as he pulled them up. He pulled her against him, wrapping one arm around her waist as he kissed her from behind. She squeezed her thighs together, savoring the warm sensation.

"That was perfect, baby girl. You're so sexy." He wrapped his arms around her, holding her close. She was still aching for him, but she closed her eyes contentedly, enjoying the hunger. It made her feel so alive and so sexy. He took her by the hand, leading her back to the sidewalk. As they walked home, she had a reminder of who she belonged to with every step.

Chapter 17

That evening, as she was getting ready for bed, she noticed that he was watching her more closely than usual.

"What is it?" she asked, finally, after catching him staring at her for the third time.

"What do you think you'd like to do now that the play is over?" he asked thoughtfully. She shrugged, caught off guard by the question.

"I don't really have a plan," she said. "I'll probably start auditioning for another role as soon as I can."

"Why don't you take some time off?" he suggested. "I'll take some time off, too, and we can take a trip somewhere."

"Seriously?" she asked, seriously considering it. "Where would we go? It was his turn to shrug as though he hadn't considered that part yet.

"Anywhere you like. Someplace tropical? The mountains, maybe?" She considered it quietly for a moment as she brushed her hair. Her head had been so wrapped up in getting her acting career going these past few years that she had never considered what kind of vacation she might like to take, and it took her a while to come to a decision.

"Someplace tropical sounds nice," she said finally. "How about Jamaica?" He grinned and nodded, getting excited at the idea.

"That's perfect. I've never been so we can both experience it for the first time together."

"I like the sound of that," she said, putting down her brush and joining him in the bed.

"Good," he said. "I'll start making the arrangements right away." She sighed and stretched, then cuddled up against him, so that he was spooning her from behind. Cuddling in that position never failed to make him horny, and tonight was no different. He brushed his fingertips lightly over her nipples, and she could feel him already getting hard against the warm swell of her buttocks. She began to grind her butt cheeks against him, already whimpering and squealing as he pinched her nipples harder, delighting in the way her eyes rolled back in her head with the heady mixture of pain and pleasure.

"I love what a greedy slut you are," he growled into her ear, one hand sliding up from her breast to her throat. He didn't apply any pressure, just held her against him like that, letting them both relish the feeling of control. After a moment, she began to squirm impatiently against him, trying to provoke a response. He tightened his hand on her throat, a tiny gasp escaping her lips. Without another word, he plunged his hard cock deep in her tight pussy, still slick with his semen, and grinned as she winced in pain and pleasure. For her, the two were inseparable now, and she yearned towards him, eager for more. He tightened his grip on her throat, delighting in the way her pussy tightened around him, and she rolled her eyes back in her head.

"That's it, baby girl. Show Daddy how dirty you like it." She tried to moan, but it came out as a muted squeak, her air-restricted by the large meaty hand wrapped around her neck. He fucked her harder, moving her hand to her clit. "Show Daddy how much you love getting fucked." She rubbed at her clit furiously, squeaking and squirming, working herself up to a climax. As he sensed she was getting close, he suddenly withdrew and released her throat, leaving her gasping and quivering.

"Not yet, kitten." He slapped her hard on the ass, leaving behind a bright pink handprint. He liked the look of it so much that he left half a dozen more, as she yelped in vain. Once again, he was overwhelmed with the feeling of being incredibly lucky to be with a woman so sexy and insatiable. She was the first woman he had ever been who could keep up with his sexual appetites and then some. "Suck Daddy's cock." The eagerness on her face as she turned herself around and sought out his erection with plump, pink lips took his breath away. As her hot mouth engulfed him, she moaned around his shaft, making him shiver with delight. He ran his fingers through her soft hair, and he sank his cock deeper into her mouth. By now, she was well trained in the art of deepthroating, so he went deeper. Once he hit her limit, she gagged but continued to pleasure him, undeterred.

"Yes, that's it. You're making Daddy's cock feel so good." She let herself get lost in pleasuring him, her favorite activity. He continued to mumble encouragement to her, wrapping her in a cocoon of safety and trust. She loved being a vessel for his pleasure, being able to express her love for him in such a tangible, physical way. She felt like she could suck his cock for hours, happily lost in a daze of submissive servitude. All too soon, however, he pulled her up from his cock by her hair. He kissed her passionately and deeply, pulling and twisting her nipples mercilessly. She writhed against him, seeking out his hardness with her aching hole, silently begging to be filled. He could sense her neediness and decided to toy with it, rubbing the head of his hard penis against her tender clit as he continued to twist and pinch her nipples. The combination turned her into a moaning, desperate thing, no longer capable of clear thought, only a bottomless pit of need that only he could fulfill. As she began to babble incoherently, lost in a fog of lust and submission, he guided her to sit on his cock, filling her at last. She sighed with deep satisfaction as he sank into her, and she wrapped her arms around his neck tightly, wanting to be even closer still. He guided her hips with his hands, and she began to ride him with abandon. He lie back, enjoying the sight of his beloved naked and uninhibited, her long hair flowing over her alabaster skin as she brought them both to the brink of ecstasy.

"Do you like that? Do you want to cum on Daddy's cock, baby girl?" he asked, already knowing the answer. He grabbed her buttocks with both hands and forced her down on his throbbing erection, filling her so deeply and completely that she almost did cum without his permission. Quivering with barely contained ecstasy, she managed to nod her head and squeak out, "Yes, Daddy." He put his thumb on her clit and thrust into her again and again, loving keeping her right on the threshold. She was so beautiful and sexy. He never wanted to stop fucking her. When he felt like he could no longer hold himself back, he gave her the command.

"Cum for me, little one." She moaned with relief, gripping his hips with her thighs and his cock with her pussy as she finally let herself go, let the climax that had been steadily building wash over. As she shook and cried out, she could feel his cock twitch as he flooded her with his hot seed. They held onto each other as the electric waves of their mutual orgasm receded, and they lie panting and sweating, tangled in one another as they slowly came back to reality. She suddenly started giggling, not even sure what was funny but so full of effervescent joy that it was spilling out of her. Much to her surprise, he too started laughing, burying his face in her neck as he held her tight against him as their bodies shook with mirth. After a moment, he kissed her gently and slid her off of him and onto the bed. Soon, they would drift off to sleep together, gathering their energy to face the world once more, side by side. For now, they were safe and content in their love nest.

Who is Tina Moore?

Tina Moore has enjoyed the lifestyle of a Mommy Domme for several years. She began exploring kink and BDSM in her youth and found her love of being a strict Mommy Domme in early 2000. Tina Moore is now an author of many MDLG, DDLG and ABDL themed novels.

Follow her on:

Author Page on Amazon

Instagram @tinamoore.kdp